The 45th Parallel

What Reviewers Say About Lisa Girolami's Work

Love on Location is… "An explosive and romantic story set in the world of movies."—*Divadirect.co.uk*

"The women of *Run to Me* are multi-dimensional and the running metaphor is well placed throughout this tale. Girolami has given us an entertaining story that makes us think—about relationships, about running away, and about what we want to run to in our lives."—*Just About Write*

"[*Jane Doe*] is one of those quiet books that ends up getting under your skin. The story flowed with the ease of a slow-moving river. All in all a well-written story with an unusual setting, and well worth the read."—*Lambda Literary Foundation*

"*Jane Doe* is a lovely, easy to read romance that left me with a smile on my face."—*Just About Write*

In *The Pleasure Set*… "Girolami has done a wonderful job portraying the wealthy dilettantes along with the complex characters of Laney and Sandrine. Her villain is a great combination of brains and ruthlessness. Of course, the sex scenes are fabulous. This novel is a great blend of sex, romance, and mystery, and the cover…is perfect."—*Just About Write*

"The highs and the lows…the soaring and the plummeting that the lovers go through is so dramatically articulated and gloriously interwoven with the tensions and difficulties besetting Los Angeles and its environs. The police scenes, the priceless moments at the refuge, the nearly unbelievable Fathers Day celebrations, the super sexy bedroom activities, plus many more elements made [*The Heat of Angels*] so bountiful, so top-notch, and so noteworthy. This extraordinary reading experience gets my highest applause and a major thumbs-up!"—*Rainbow Book Reviews*

By the Author

Love on Location

Run to Me

The Pleasure Set

Jane Doe

Fugitives of Love

Cut to the Chase

The Heat of Angels

The 45th Parallel

The 45th Parallel

by

Lisa Girolami

2015

THE 45TH PARALLEL

ISBN 13: 978-1-62639-342-4

This Trade Paperback Original Is Published By
Bold Strokes Books, Inc.
P.O. Box 249
Valley Falls, NY 12185

First Edition: May 2015

Credits
Editor: Shelley Thrasher
Production Design: Susan Ramundo
Cover Design By Sheri (graphicartist2020@hotmail.com)

Acknowledgments

To the unnamed real town that inspired this tome, I thank you for your wind-swept history, your sun-dappled stories, and your wonderfully salty citizens.

Shelley Thrasher, you're my unsung hero.

Cindy Cresap, you're my tenacious conscience.

Rad, you're my fearless Alpha.

My readers, you're all my treasured motivation.

Dedication

For my angel, my supporter, my silly girl, my partner in crime, my rock, my brave and amazing wife, Kari.

CHAPTER ONE

Sheets of Oregon coastal mist built up on the windshield, mixing the larger blots of vaporized bugs into watery smudges. The wetness obstructed Val Montague's view until a few swift swipes of her wipers pushed the deposits out of the way.

She turned the wiper blades off and wished she were anywhere but here.

Though Val knew this road better than the ones within five miles of her house back in Dallas, an uneasy tightness in her chest bent her forward and she squinted, old-grumpy-woman-like, into the dark night. She couldn't trust that there wasn't a new turn in the road or potholes that could quickly and unexpectedly blow out a tire on her mother's car.

She'd flown into the Portland airport that night and taken a cab to Legacy Good Samaritan Hospital where, thanks to the understanding security people who'd held on to the keys and watched it for her until she could get there, her mother's car had been waiting.

The politely solemn faces of the two security men who handed her the keys reminded her that she didn't need to go inside the hospital. Her mother wasn't there anymore.

It was well past one o'clock in the morning, and prickles of frustration poked her neck like scratchy clothing tags. She didn't want to be traveling so late, but the only flight she could arrange had connected more times than a teenager on a cell phone. Being the only person on the road also bothered her, and worse than that, she'd get into town in the middle of the night and have to fumble around an old house whose silence would undoubtedly scream loudly in her ears.

She inhaled deeply and felt more tired than she should. Memories that had occupied her since she'd left on this trip closed in around her like wet woolen blankets intended to warm her but, instead, only weighed her down further. Twenty years was a long time to be gone. She'd spent almost half her life living as far away from this place as she could, but the familiarity of the old road served as an apprehensive preamble to a timeworn book she was reluctant to open again.

Just as she remembered, the Oregon Highway 101 South was still narrow, with the same faded lines and crumbling, irregular edges. Even through the haze of the night, her headlights corroborated her memories of the long rides between her childhood home and anywhere else. The particulars of this stretch hadn't changed much in the last two decades. The forest corridor was still as isolated as ever, with the only evidence of life being a deer or two foraging along the side or the approaching or receding pairs of headlights that became very infrequent this late at night.

The trees were dense on either side of the road though, and if it were daytime, she would see patches of the ocean appearing in the thinner spots to the right. A long-ago disregarded cabin, crusted with Oregon moss, indicated that she was six miles from town. It still sat empty, looking exactly the same, although it seemed now to lean a little farther away from the road, as if it were slowly falling asleep. Or dying.

After another mile the road curved, still tracking the ocean, and she swiped the wipers once more to clear the dampness from the windshield. She searched for the next familiar marker and found it. The arrow-shaped sign pointing summer tourists to the public-beach parking lot was still there. But it wasn't summer so the sign sat, neglected and ignored, much like she knew her mother would have felt during the last years of her life.

From out of the murky fog in front of her, brake lights began as dim red dots and grew larger and brighter. As she caught up to the slow-moving, late-model Buick, the wet reflection of its red taillights on the misty road stretched toward her like arms reaching for help. She tapped the brakes until she was about six car-lengths behind and close enough to see a sticker on the bumper. She leaned forward to read it through the wet windshield. LAND YOUR BOW AT DORY COVE RESTAURANT.

She'd eaten there many times as a child. They had the best plate of fish and chips a kid could ever dig into.

Val held her distance on the road, aware that the potentially perilous conditions of the dark, drizzly highway called for her to mimic the pace of the Buick.

It was odd to see a car out this late. When she'd lived here, the road would become desolate after dark. Tourists would already be where they were heading, and the locals would be home for the night. Maybe the Buick had been ahead of her all the way from the airport, but since turning onto Highway 101, she hadn't seen anyone out on the road. And there weren't many side roads this car could have turned out from.

What did it matter, she thought. Just like it didn't matter that she stay so vigilant, worrying that the road was any different than the thousand times she'd driven down it as a child.

A few miles ahead would be the turnoff for Venom Lake, the popular spot for the locals who wanted to stay clear of the saltwater-loving tourists, and then just past that, the dim lights of the first buildings that marked the northern point of the small beach town. Hardly two miles in length, Hemlock, Oregon hung onto the ocean's edge, as if waiting for something more exciting than wind erosion to liven things up.

Another sign approached and she almost laughed as she remembered it. The green highway sign, with its white, prismatic reflecting letters, read THE 45TH PARALLEL. HALFWAY BETWEEN THE EQUATOR AND THE NORTH POLE.

She shook her head, remembering that she'd once asked her mom what that meant.

"Well, we're halfway between the Equator and the North Pole."

"Why is that important?" Val had said, not understanding the meaning.

"It's a special marker. We live halfway between two remarkable places, so that makes us remarkable."

"But why would that make us remarkable?" She'd been only about ten at the time, but she knew enough about how boring life was in Hemlock and wondered how this sign made it any different.

"Because no one else around here can claim that. You can stand right here and you're exactly halfway, Val. Hemlock is pretty special because of that."

"And that's why they have the Halfway Festival?"

Her mother took her to the event every summer. Tourists would crowd the beach, buying halfway hamburgers and 45th sodas that the Chamber of Commerce would hawk while one of the local churches would play music and hold a raffle.

"Yes, dear. It brings people to Hemlock, which we need. We live on summer tourist dollars. That's how we make it through the slow winters."

That was about the gist of the conversation, but it had never made sense to her. Claiming a place was noteworthy because it happened to lie halfway between two noteworthy places didn't seem to make Hemlock any more important. In her ten-year-old mind, maybe Hemlock was amazing compared to the rest of the non-45th parallel towns. What did she know? She'd never been anywhere else.

As she passed the sign, Val now knew that Hemlock certainly was not more amazing than anywhere else. The Chamber of Commerce milked the moniker to draw in tourist dollars. Local businesses sold 45th parallel T-shirts, and if it was still there, a coffee shop was called the 45th Parallel Pantry. Even the sports teams of her tiny local school were called the Forty-Fivers.

It began to rain, which wasn't unusual, so she turned the windshield wipers back on.

Squinting at the view ahead, she followed the Buick past the more darkened trees, and again she sighed. Her emotional internal battle continued. She didn't want to come back, but she had to. Regret arm-wrestled with grief and the resulting knots tied up her stomach. Her eyes felt as heavy as bowling balls crammed inside her orbital sockets.

She reached up and rubbed her eyes, but in the second that her hand blocked her view of the road, she saw a flash of red. The Buick suddenly swerved, and its brake lights cut terrifying red slashes through the rainy night.

A surge of adrenaline shot through her, and she grabbed the steering wheel just as the Buick's back end bucked upward and the tires skidded frantically on the wet road. In a split second something flew over the Buick's hood and over the top of the car.

Val stomped on her brakes and went into her own skid as a huge brown object flew toward her. In the quarter of a second it was airborne, Val could see it was a deer and cringed as it smashed into her front grill and bounced grotesquely onto her hood and into the windshield. She closed her eyes and threw an arm up as she stomped harder on her brakes. The screeching of her wheels against the rain-slick road sounded like a scream as the deer careened off Val's car, and then, just as quickly, everything went silent.

"Fuck!" she finally said as she grasped her keys and tried to steady her shaking hand so she could turn off the engine.

The sudden stillness chilled her. The reptilian preservation portion of her brain let go of its momentary total dominance, and, as her body caught up with the rest of her thoughts, she gasped harshly for air.

Her hood was as crushed as her windshield, and through the spider web of safety glass, she saw that her car had come to rest just a few feet from the Buick.

Jumping out, she turned in the direction of the deer but couldn't see it. A woman got out of her car and stood by the door. She couldn't have been more than six feet away, and her eyes were as wide as her brake lights.

Val took a few steps toward her. "Are you all right?"

"I think so. I'm not sure what happened."

"You hit a deer. We hit a deer."

The young woman stood there staring at her.

"Are you sure you're okay?"

The woman rubbed her forehead. "Yeah. It just scared the hell out of me."

Val turned to inspect her grill, hearing the wet footsteps of the woman as she walked up to her. The damage was pretty extensive. The grill was crushed into the pleated hood, and luminous greenish-yellow fluid poured from the bottom.

"Antifreeze," the woman said.

The car most likely wasn't drivable. She wouldn't make it to town without the car overheating and causing more damage than she cared to report to the insurance agency.

Val's hands still shook, and she clenched them to persuade blood to begin to flow again. The bushes and trees along the side of the road were motionless. She took a step toward them.

"Hey." The word stuttered out of the woman in three syllables. "Where are you going?"

"To find the deer."

"What if it's still alive? It could charge you. I wouldn't go looking for it."

"I doubt it'll be in any shape to charge."

Val slowly walked around the backside of her car. The young woman followed closely behind. It was too dark to see much, but Val suddenly stopped.

"There." She pointed as the woman craned her neck. About forty feet down the road, off in the tall grass next to the tree line, the deer lay in a hump. It was a little too far to see if it was breathing, and it made no noise. The only sounds came from the spattering of raindrops on the pavement and murky, black leaves beyond, and the eerie creaking of trees. Standing in the rain, in the dark, creeped her out. She wanted to shake off the shudders that threatened to make her jerk like an ill-treated marionette. Instead she rubbed her hands together again.

"He's dead," the woman said.

Val stared at the deer, watching for a twitch or some sign of life. The woman was right; it could be dangerous to approach it. But they'd both just hit the poor thing. Slowly, she took a step and the woman blurted out, "It's off the road."

"Geez!" Val jumped.

"Sorry. But that's all the rangers and highway patrol care about."

Even if the deer were alive, if it hadn't yet gotten up or started thrashing about, it was probably dead.

"Shit." Reaching into her pocket, she said, "I've got a cell phone. I'll call the highway patrol."

"No," the woman said hastily. "I wouldn't do that." She hesitated. "It'll be a long wait. And there's only one Hemlock officer working at night. He won't come up past Venom Lake on his shift."

Val looked at her for an explanation.

The woman just shrugged. "Lazy."

The rain began to pick up; the cold drops made her shake more.

"You're gonna need a tow truck."

Resigned, Val nodded. "Yours too?"

She jerked her head toward the Buick. "Yeah, bummer. I think Mack's the only one that'll come out here this late."

"Who's Mack?"

"One of the two mechanics we have in town." She pointed to where they were both heading prior to the accident.

"Does he have a tow truck?"

The young woman closed her jacket tighter and nodded.

Great, Val thought as disappointment joined the rest of the unpleasant feelings she'd been dealing with. This would add time to a visit she really needed to be as short as possible.

CHAPTER TWO

The woman stood along the side of the road with Val until the tow truck came. Val considered sitting in the car to keep out of the rain, but the girl made no move to do the same and Val was already soaked, so they remained there, not saying much. Luckily, they waited only fifteen minutes or so, and Val supposed that was one of the few good things about a small town.

A tall, lanky man climbed out of a tow truck that had probably assisted many Studebakers and Edsels in its youth. He was at least forty, although it was hard to tell because the sun and, more than likely, smoking or drinking hadn't been too kind to his looks.

Though he gave the truck door quite a push, it didn't close all the way but just clunked against the frame and creaked its way back out a few inches.

"Evenin', Cindy."

"Hey, Mack. This here's…" Cindy turned to Val. "I didn't get your name."

"Val. Montague."

Mack looked at her in that you're-not-from-around-here squint. "Miss Montague's kid?"

"Kris Montague, yes."

"My condolences."

"Thank you."

Mack started to hitch up Val's car. "Cindy, I'll take you and drop you off and then come back for your car after, okay?"

"Yeah."

When he was done, he motioned for Cindy and her to get in the truck. "Come on, it's a short ride."

It was short but not quiet. Val assumed that every part on the truck was loose. Things clanked and squeaked and hissed with such a cadence that it sounded as if a dreadfully unrehearsed orchestra was warming up.

They didn't talk at all except for Mack sucking what must have been dinner from his teeth. And from what his coveralls revealed, dinner was probably ribs and mashed potatoes. She began to wonder what kind of moonshine he washed it all down with but stopped and silently scolded herself for having disparaging thoughts. She didn't have any reason to cop an attitude. She should be grateful he'd come to help, for God sakes.

She looked out the rain-slicked window, watching the population of little buildings and houses grow. And there it was. The Hemlock town-limit sign. The population was the same, 3,858 people, which either meant that since she left, no one had come or gone but her, or that the town just didn't care to spend the funds to update the sign.

She didn't see any new houses or commercial buildings, but everything was dark along the street. She recognized the liquor store, the Bijou Theater, and the smattering of closed-for-the-season souvenir shops whose neon signs were all turned off. The tow truck slowed down, and Val looked up to see the only lit sign in town. It read simply BOB MACKINAW, MECHANIC.

Cindy had been right. Mack was probably the only person who was even moving about this late at night.

Val sat with Cindy in the front waiting room of the converted gas station. The chairs stood in a row and each one was different from the other, as if they'd been picked up at thrift stores here and there and deposited without much thought. Hers had a gold metal frame and a vinyl seat with an autumn-leaves motif. It had obviously spent its previous life in a 1960s kitchen. Cindy slouched back in a wicker lawn chair that seemed to be desperately holding on to its last bit of red, sun-worn paint. But every time Cindy adjusted her butt, a small chip or two would dislodge and fall to the floor under her.

Mack had given them Styrofoam cups of coffee that tasted like the bottom of a muddy river, but Val was appreciative. She hoped it wouldn't take that long to assess the damage. Fatigue had crept into her shoulders and head, and she really needed to get some sleep.

Mack must have called in a helper because another mechanic was in the shop. He'd been waiting at the garage when they'd returned and had hopped in the tow truck as soon as Mack had backed in and unhooked Val's car. Now he was back with Cindy's car and they were examining the damage.

Val listened to the sounds coming from the garage. Doors opened and closed, and the cries of metal creaking meant that Mack was probably examining their hoods.

Cindy was on her phone playing some game with fruit being slashed into mushy pieces. She didn't seem concerned about her car's damage and the possible costs involved. She was young enough that it might have been her parents' car, but she didn't look worried about their reaction either.

Val stood and paced the front room. A water dispenser stood in the corner, the large plastic bottle on top filled with what looked like pink lemonade. A sign taped to the big jug read For our littlest customers only.

She checked her watch and then opened the door into the garage area. Cindy jumped out of her chair and was immediately behind her. Maybe the fruit war had only temporarily kept her concern about the car's damage at bay.

Mack walked around the cars writing things down on a clipboard. The other mechanic, who wasn't as tall as Mack but very wide and muscular, shuffled around in the background.

Mack stopped at Val's car and reached down, under the bent hood. He put the clipboard down and retrieved a crowbar from a nearby workbench, then pried the hood open as far as he could. Peering in, he nodded and returned to the clipboard.

He walked back to them, speaking to Cindy first. "You've got some front-end damage. Your car's drivable, but you should get a new hood and grill."

He handed the estimate to her and looked at his clipboard again. Val followed him over to her car.

"Your windshield's cracked, as you can see. The deer hit the top portion of your hood and grill. The radiator needs replacing and so does the windshield."

"Is it drivable?"

"No. You wouldn't get far with that broken radiator." He handed her the estimate.

"I need to call my mother's insurance agency in Portland and see what they say. How long will you need to have the car?" Either way, Val thought, she'd probably still have to rent a car.

"I'll have to call about the availability of a radiator. But it shouldn't be long at all since it's a newer model. Too late to call now. I'll know tomorrow. I'll need your keys."

She pulled the car key from the keychain and dropped it into Mack's open hand.

"Bobby," Mack called out to the other mechanic. "Drive these women home, will ya?"

It was after two in the morning when Bobby turned off Coast Highway and drove the three hundred feet up her mom's street and dropped Val off in front of the house. He didn't wait to see her get in safely, but that was fine with her. She wasn't sure she even wanted to go in.

Standing next to her rolling suitcase, she paused and listened to the sound of distant waves from the ocean. She closed her eyes and felt the cool, damp sea air on her face, letting herself be carried back to her childhood. She turned her head away from the ocean, and the ever-present scent of pines greeted her like one of the few friends she had that had ever brought her tranquility. As far back as she could remember, any time of the day, she could always close her eyes and just breathe in. The evergreens would take her away to the forest and she could picture herself all alone, with no arguing, no craving to be chosen over her mother's boyfriends, and no heartache.

Opening her eyes, she told herself that she no longer needed to escape. She'd already accomplished that feat. She was just back temporarily to take care of things and leave.

She searched the yard for the for-sale sign and found it in the southern-most corner, close to the street. NEDRA TOBIAS REAL ESTATE, it read, NOT THE ONLY AGENT IN TOWN. JUST THE BEST. She didn't know Nedra other than hearing her mother mention her once or twice during their infrequent phone calls. She was a friend, part of the same church her mother attended, she thought, but wasn't sure.

Jingling her mother's keychain, she took one more deep breath of pine air and walked up the three porch steps to unlock the door.

She closed the door behind her and let go of the suitcase. The house was as neat as she remembered. To the right of the foyer was the living room, very quaint, with warm, inviting furniture. The dining room was off to the left, leading to the kitchen. In front of her, the hallway ran width-wise and led to a bathroom straight ahead and two bedrooms; her mother's was on the left, hers had been on the right.

Val walked into the dining room. How many meals had she eaten at this very table? How many meals had she been excused from and sent to her room?

She walked into the living room and plopped down on the couch. She'd always appreciated her mother's simple taste. No tchotchkes filled up every space like they had in the homes of her friends' parents. Most things that were displayed had a meaning or a purpose. An Aleutian Eskimo had given her mother the small handwoven basket neatly centered on the coffee table, small enough to fit daintily in her palm when she was a young girl.

Three beautifully carved wooden faces hung on the wall across from her. Each was painted in elaborate Kabuki makeup and represented the three kanji symbols that made up the word for the classical Japanese dance-drama: song, dance, and skill. Her mother had brought it home from a trip to Japan, long before Val was born, when she had spent a summer in Kyoto, the place of origin of the art form.

On the end table, next to her mother's reading chair, sat a miniature bronze figurine of a rabbit that had accompanied her mother home from Austria. Its Art-Deco lines had always intrigued Val, although her mother's description of the style as Streamline Moderne had been too hard for a little girl to remember. But Art Deco reminded her of artwork on a wooden deck, much like the wooden table on which it always rested, so it was easier to remember the style that way.

Her mother had traveled extensively before marrying Val's father, but she had no global artifacts from her post-marriage years. Either her father had made her mother stop traveling or the arrival of Val had. Either way, it always made Val sad to think that her mother had a life before her family and a different, possibly disappointing, kind of life after.

Val looked up toward the ceiling. The paint had very slightly yellowed, but maybe it was just the lighting. Either way, the house would soon be sold and, along with it, all the memories of her childhood. She could look at that as either good or bad, depending on what she chose to focus on.

But she decided to quit reminiscing for the night. It was very late and she had things to do tomorrow.

"Mom," she said aloud, "I'm sorry about selling this place. And about your car."

She wheeled her suitcase into her old bedroom. The bed was made and the sheets weren't musty, so all she had to do was brush her teeth, undress, and get some sleep.

She reached in her pants pocket and retrieved her mother's keychain. The brass house key was worn to a shine on the tiny jagged mountain peaks that had to have been inserted into the front door hundreds of thousands of times. The car key was with Mack, and the only other key on the ring was thin and had a longer neck. It looked like a safe-deposit-box key. She had another errand to run.

Suddenly very tired, she placed her hands over her face. Her sigh helped alleviate absolutely none of the heaviness in her heart.

❖

Unable to sleep, Val awoke very early. She recalled bizarre-feeling dreams whose images and themes had vanished with the amnesia of sleep, leaving her disturbed and tired. She lay awake for a long time, reviewing the tasks that lay ahead. Finally around seven, she got up and took a shower.

Now in the kitchen, she poured coffee into a mug and looked out the window. The morning was fresh and crisp. But the Oregon coast had swept a light layer of fog across the lawn and it hovered there, as if loitering about, waiting for something or someone. The kitchen was in the corner of the house, so she could see the coastal highway. Her mother's street ran perpendicular to the highway. Though her mom's house was the third house in, she couldn't quite see the water because of the buildings across the way. But it was there, less than sixty feet behind the structures. A few cars traversed back and forth on the highway, and none seemed in a hurry.

A brand-new red Tesla slowed at the corner and came up toward the house. Val watched it park in front and wondered who it was.

An elderly woman climbed out, adjusted her business dress, and then walked up to the for-sale sign. She regarded it momentarily and reached out to straighten it. She brushed off a few pine needles from the wooden post and, when she appeared satisfied, turned toward the walkway and approached the house. Evidently, this was Nedra Tobias.

Val, cup in hand, was already opening the front door when the bell rang.

"Oh," Nedra said, obviously surprised. She was about as old as her mother but much more well dressed. Maybe that was because Nedra had a job that required it. Her mother was retired and hadn't needed to make the extra effort. "Good morning," Nedra said. "I see your flight got in on time. Did you have any trouble finding your way back to our gem of a little town?

"Just some car trouble, but nothing to worry about."

The comment didn't seem to register because Nedra was already saying, "Valerie Montague! My, my, have you grown! You were a beautiful young lady when you left and now look at you! Your mother in heaven is very proud of you."

Val slowly cocked her head. "I'm sorry, but I don't remember ever…"

Nedra waved the rest of the comment away as if it were a troublesome gnat. "Your mother has shown me many pictures of you. Back when you were in high school, of course."

"Uh," Val said. Her discomfort that this woman probably knew more about her mother than Val did made her uneasy. "Thank you. Would you like to come in for some coffee?"

"No, thank you, honey. I'm off to the office. I just wanted to stop by and confirm the open house today."

"Ten o'clock, right?"

"Yes, ten until two. Now I'll be here to watch your things. We're bonded. All the good agents are, you know. The owners don't normally stay, you know. It makes potential buyers nervous. They like to be able to talk openly. You understand…"

Nedra patted her on the wrist as she continued. "I'm so sorry your mother died, Valerie. Kris was a good woman. She's been irreplaceable at church. I'll make sure this home gets a decent owner."

"Thank you," she said. "Nedra, may I ask you something?"

"Sure, dear, what is it?"

"Do you know what happened the night my mom got sick and went to the hospital?"

"Well, not exactly. I heard she went to the hospital, and then they called the police station when they found out she lived in Hemlock. I read about it in the local paper."

"The doctor at the emergency room said she must have been having trouble because she drove herself to the hospital. He said she died of sudden arrhythmic death."

"I know. I'm so sorry. It was awful."

"Had you noticed that she was having any trouble breathing, or was she complaining of dizziness?" Val had researched the condition on the Internet, which explained for her that arrhythmia must have caused her mom's heart rhythm to go out of synch and that it had either been beating too fast or too slow. Certainly cancer and diabetes had plagued her older relatives, but no one had ever had heart problems.

"No, she didn't say anything to me about that."

"Do you know if she'd been to the doctor recently?"

"She might have, but we never talked about it." Nedra picked a small piece of peeling paint from the doorframe. "I sure wish you'd move back here, Val. I could find you another place…maybe up the coast a little ways—"

"Thank you, but no, Nedra. I'll stay until everything's liquidated, and then I'll be getting back to Dallas."

"Is the antique business going well, dear?"

She did know more than Val had assumed. "Yes. I travel quite a bit and I enjoy it."

"Must be exciting!"

"Nedra," Val said, "do you think it'll take long? For the house to sell, I mean."

"I don't suppose so. Kris kept this house up very nicely. And beach property is always at a premium. Plus, I know everyone in town, and I've sold most of the houses in Hemlock at least once."

Val leaned out the door, looking toward her neighbors. "It's a small house compared to these others."

Again, she waved off Val's words. "It doesn't matter, dear. Big houses, small houses. They all sell well when you've practically got sand for a backyard."

"Okay, thank you."

Nedra turned to walk back to her car. "Don't worry about a thing. I'll take care of all the details."

Val stood at the open door a few minutes after Nedra had motored off in a car that seemed so out of the ordinary for a small, backward town.

She thought about her mother and wondered if anything could have saved her. It all had to have happened pretty quickly, and Val felt the wretched pain of knowing she died alone.

A bright-blue Kia rounded the corner, shaking Val from her thoughts. When it parked in front of her house, she knew this was the rental car she'd called for. They'd told her they'd deliver it and all she had to do was sign a few papers and drop the driver back off at the agency down in Newport.

The distant cackling of a seagull sounded from the direction of the ocean. She used to chase them when she was a kid, running up and down that same beach for hours, convinced that she'd eventually catch one.

A chapter was truly closing. She'd never had a chance to come back home and relive her childhood. And now that she was back, she didn't seem to have enough time, or desire, to do so.

Val sat in a claustrophobically small, plain gray-wallpapered room the size of her chair plus about six inches on all sides. The bank teller checked her ID, verified her mother's death certificate, and led her into the vault. She showed her how they both had to open the numbered vault door with two keys to access the safe-deposit box and then walked her to the room before handing her the box and closing the door behind her.

The safe-deposit box sat on a diminutive table in front of her. She ran her finger down its cool, metal side. The last time someone had touched this box, her mother had been alive. She thought to look for telltale fingerprints, but what good would that do? She couldn't take the prints home with her as a keepsake. Still, she felt closer knowing her mother had probably sat in this same room, in the same chair, looking at the same box.

She lifted the lid and peered inside. A large manila envelope and a small, white envelope with a paper-clipped note attached lay inside.

She took a deep breath, full of melancholy, and opened the note.

Dearest Val,

I know one day you'll be sitting here reading this. That means I'm now gone. This is for you. It's not much, but you're my only child and it's all yours. The lawyers told me that a living trust is the best way to ensure that you receive the most possible from my estate.

Love, Mom.

Val opened the white envelope.

In her mother's handwriting, it read, CREMAINS WISHES. She stared at the first line. How had it felt, writing about yourself being dead? There was an address of a mortuary and directions to a place up the Siletz River.

She hadn't been there since she was a kid and her mother would take her for drives there. It wasn't until junior-high school that she found out the reason for the infrequent one-on-one time: her mother had needed to get away from whatever asshole boyfriend was living with them at the time.

Val would tell her mother how she wished they lived right on the river so they could sit and watch the water roll by on its way to the ocean.

The note with the directions made Val's chest ache and her eyes fill with tears. She blinked them away, watching a few drip from her cheeks and splash onto the note like the beginning storm warnings of an unwelcome cloudburst.

She closed the note and then opened the manila envelope. Flipping through the numerous pages of the thick living-trust document, she realized she wasn't absorbing any of it. Her thoughts were still in her mom's car on the road that wound along the curvy Siletz River as she wondered how the hell she ever got from there to here. Her eyes registered the black words on the white linen paper, but nothing was intelligible.

Suddenly, she felt like she hadn't slept in weeks. Her arms were heavy and her eyes wouldn't focus. Slowly, she slid the living trust back into the manila envelope. She'd read it later, she decided. Putting it under her arm, she got up and walked out.

❖

Hemlock had always been too small to support a mortuary so Val drove down to an address in Newport. The fairly sunny ocean-side ride was pleasant, though the mission was certainly not.

Quietus Mortuary was easy to find. It was a serious-looking building of brick and white trim and had none of the gratuitous flourishes that would call attention to itself. Sitting stoically between a real-estate office, which was selling the best of the Oregon coast, and a flower shop, whose strategically chosen location was obvious, it looked solemn without appearing dismal.

Soft music played in the lobby, and Val waited there until she heard muted footsteps coming down the carpeted hall.

"May I help you?" An older gentleman, dressed in a gray three-piece suit and black loafers, bore the kind of thoughtful expression and soft voice Val always pictured that a person of that profession would have. She almost wished he'd been rougher around the edges and had a snarky attitude, because her throat immediately tightened and she was afraid she might run into his protective-looking arms and cry her eyes out.

"Yes, I'm Valerie Montague," she said, hoping that concentrating on simply fulfilling the task at hand would save her from thinking any deeper than she wanted to. "I am here to…pick my mother up."

"Certainly," he said. "Kris Montague, is that correct?"

Val nodded.

"I'm William Boswell, Director of Quietus." He offered his hand and Val shook it.

"Please come with me."

Val followed him to a small office designed expressly for grieving families. There was nothing showy about the room, and Val thought it was decorated rather well, offering a comfortable place to discuss the uncomfortable business of death.

"Please sit down." He gestured to a plush but modest couch sitting against the wall between two rather sizeable flower urns.

He didn't sit but excused himself and left the office. The wallpaper was a mauve color with tiny flowers and vertical gold pinstripes. On the wall hung two oceanscapes, one taken in the early morning and the other at dusk. Were they meant to suggest the passing of time, or maybe the passing of people?

Like her mom, she thought, fighting back a grape-sized lump that caught in her throat. And then something occurred to her. If she was handling her mother's pickup, who had dealt with her arrival?

Mr. Boswell returned with some paperwork and a container the size of a square box of Kleenex.

"First of all," he said as he sat down at his desk, "I am very sorry for your loss." He flipped through the paperwork. "Your mother left instructions to be cremated."

When he gently patted the box, Val stared, wondering how her mother could fit in such a small space.

"Her lawyer contacted us and gave us those instructions. They're here in the paperwork we'll release to you."

Her mother was gone, and though she wondered certain things like who knew to contact the lawyer and who drove her here, the answers now seemed as insignificant as what her mom had for breakfast on her last day. She had so many questions about her death, but the answers wouldn't help her feel any better. The details didn't really matter.

Mr. Boswell went over the paperwork and, after verifying Val's identity, handed her the file and the box of cremains, then walked her to the door.

Now in her car, driving back to Hemlock, she checked her watch. The open house wouldn't be over until two o'clock, so she still had two hours before returning to her mother's place. What would she do to fill the gap?

"Well, Mom," Val said to the box sitting on the seat next to her. "Here we are. I imagine when you pictured my coming back here to visit, it didn't look quite like this."

She drove north and slowed her car as she reached the south end of Hemlock, where the few tourists that did choose to vacation during October were flying kites on the beach. A colorful octopus with long flowing tendrils chased two fat ladybugs high over the sand, while an immense yellow-and-black bumblebee cavorted above the waves. The kites, as well as their pilots, looked so carefree and happy. The ocean breeze seemed delighted to lift the plastic critters and take them for a cheerful ride, while her own ride was anything but.

She reached over and placed her hand on the box. "I'm sorry, Mom." Tears suddenly flowed and she cried for the next few blocks. When her vision became blurry, she pulled over to the curb, in front of a T-shirt shop, and turned off the engine.

Luckily, a past renter had left a small travel-size package of Kleenex in the glove compartment. She opened the package and wiped her eyes with a few sheets, pushing them into her face because the pressure seemed to relieve the onset of a dull but rapidly intruding headache.

She found nothing enjoyable about this day or this trip. Not that she'd expected it to be festive, but now that she was in the middle of it, her sadness completely engulfed every part of her, attacking every cell inside her like an unwelcomed flu. Her bones hurt, and she was suddenly more exhausted than she could ever recall being. Even the sight of those beautiful kites didn't bring any lightness to her heart.

She remained there for quite a while, just letting the traffic pass her by like so many of the missed opportunities in her life.

She should have had better contact with her mother. She should have made peace with the frustration that had lived inside her right after graduation. She should have forgiven herself for leaving town with hardly a good-bye to anyone. And while she was at it, she should have slowed down when she reached Texas and gotten to know a few of the women she was so good at running from.

She'd hit the pavement in Dallas with two goals. She had to support herself and never end up second fiddle again. Her mother had pushed her to the back in favor of her boyfriends and their various sources of income, and while she knew that her mother was only trying to survive after her husband left, Val was still that kid that needed to stay out of the way.

So when Val began meeting single available women in Dallas, she'd tried dating them and even lived with two. But she just couldn't trust that something or someone else wouldn't come along and drive her to the back again.

Val took a deep breath and slapped herself lightly on the cheek. This pity party wasn't doing her any good. A few extra Kleenexes and a check in the rearview mirror seemed to wrap up her brief collapse. She took a deep breath, blew it out noisily, and checked her watch.

She had another hour and forty-five minutes to kill.

A walk down the street seemed like a good way to change her state of mind. She locked the car and strolled down the block. The most she was able to do was window-shop and peruse last season's inventory of souvenirs, beach blankets, and T-shirts. A few blocks down, though, the kite shop was open for business. Maybe surrounding herself with bright colors and vacationers would smother a little of her gloom.

But when she walked into the store, she saw kids with moms and dads, and they were all laughing and oohing and ahhing as they frolicked around the aisles. Val stepped backward and out of the store, doubting that anything there could make her feel better.

Walking away from the kite place, she shook her head in frustration. This sensitivity thing was getting way out of hand. Maybe she should find a bar, order anything that was a deep-caramel color and drink it straight.

Man, she was messed up. She had her mother in a box on the front seat, a house filled with childhood memories to sell, and she'd killed a deer.

With that triple downer to contend with, what the hell was her key to salvation? Val looked up and, suddenly, it was obvious.

Saltwater taffy.

Chapter Three

When Val walked into Oregon Coastal Confections, the sweet and warming scent of melted sugar was so thick she was probably ingesting calories with each breath. If she'd seen a bucket of free money right in front of her, she'd have easily passed it by to get to the front counter.

Val was staring so intently at the scrumptious chocolate shapes lining the shelves of the glass counter, she thought one of the pecan turtles had spoken to her.

"Afternoon."

Val looked up to the shopkeeper and quickly said, "Hello."

The woman was about Val's height and maybe thirty-six or thirty-seven years old. Her hair was black and curled just slightly as it came to rest on her shoulders. She was smiling at her.

The woman's eyes fascinated Val. They were of such a pale-blue color they appeared gray. Maybe it was the slate-colored tight shirt she was wearing that played with her eyes, but whatever it was, Val had seen eyes that intense only once, though she couldn't remember when.

"Take your time," the woman said, and began placing chocolate-dipped Oreo cookies on one of the shelves.

Val nodded and slowly walked around the shop ogling the bins of candy and taffy and shelves covered with vintage candy and European delights. The walls were like museum displays dedicated to every candy ever produced.

"This is incredible," Val said.

"I want to be known as *the* candy shop, not just some candy shop."

Val stood and surveyed the absolutely amazing assortment. "Wax lips, Necco wafers. Wow, candy cigarettes."

"Sales have gone up since they outlawed them in bars."

Val looked up, the question *really* forming on her lips, but the woman's smile stopped her. She chuckled and went back to relishing the inventory.

"That's the biggest Almond Joy bar I've ever seen."

"One pound of chocolate, almonds, and coconut. In terms of pure bliss, that horse hits the trifecta."

"And, at that size, it's triple the sugar buzz."

"Yeah, but what a way to go."

This time Val laughed. A few more steps brought her to another display.

"I haven't seen Pixie Stix in years." The taste of the paper came right back to her as she remembered when, as a kid, she'd bite into the striped straw and rip the top off. "They still make them?"

"Yup," the woman said. "The philosophy is not only well proven but wise. When chewing becomes too much of an effort, you can just tip your head back and mainline the sugar."

"Oh, how many summer days I spent in a candy coma from those things."

"They're still just as potent, so be careful."

All of the merchandise left little room in the store for walking or anything else, but who wanted an empty candy store? Making her way over to the chocolate counter, the woman pulled out a pleated paper cup and offered it to her.

"Try this."

Val took the paper cup and noticed it held a square piece of milk chocolate. "What is it?"

"Well, mostly it's an experiment. It's a chocolate-covered piece of coffee cake I made with brown sugar, cinnamon, and Mexican vanilla extract."

Val hadn't heard the last few words because what greeted her mouth was so incredibly amazing that her brain exploded in her ears.

"Oh, my God," she managed to say.

"Unlike the ease of Pixie Stix, you still have to chew, though."

"I know, but who cares? This is fantastic."

"Thanks."

"No, really. This is beyond words."

"I'm still testing different batches, but I hope to have them for sale within the week."

"I'd say you're done testing." Val pointed to her mouth. "This is like chocolate heroin."

"Hmm," the woman said.

Her smile was so engaging that Val suddenly felt like the only other person in the world. The sensation both delighted and alarmed her.

"I was just thinking about calling it that, too."

"You were?" Val had never been hypnotized before but it might be happening now. Shouldn't it involve a swinging pocket watch or something?

"No. But I'll take that as a compliment."

"You should. I may have to order a few kilos."

Val studied the rest of the candy on the glass shelves.

"Got a sweet tooth," the shopkeeper said, "or are you looking for a gift?"

"Definitely a sweet tooth."

"What looks good?"

She considered one type of candy, then another, and finally looked up at the woman, smiling. "I can't decide."

"How about starting with our fundamental and essential offering?" The shopkeeper came around from behind the counter and over to an area filled with counters full of buckets of saltwater candy.

"That's another treat I haven't had since I was young."

"You probably didn't have this flavor back then." She handed Val a piece.

When she tasted it, she paused. "What is this?"

"Cheesecake."

"Wow."

She pointed around to the different bins. "We have our standards—vanilla, banana, apple, and cinnamon. And then we have our more extreme flavors like amaretto, rhubarb, bubblegum, jalapeño, and even habanero."

"Do you make them?"

She tilted her head. "Back there, in the corner."

A large copper kettle sat next to a marble shelf, and a pull machine was attached to the wall. It looked almost magical.

"Is it hard to make?"

"Not really, just a little time consuming. After I melt all the ingredients the taffy has to be pulled to add air to the corn syrup and sugar. So I drape ten or fifteen pounds over that hook on the wall. The taffy starts to stretch. When it's about five or six feet long, I place it on the puller that loops the taffy back over and folds onto itself. The air that's trapped in between helps to keep the taffy soft. After that, I roll it by hand, cut it, and wrap up the pieces."

"That's quite an undertaking."

"That's because my taffy's special. It contains rather formidable powers." She handed Val a basket and said, "The first handful's on me."

"I couldn't do that—"

"You look like you could use some down-home, good ol' sugar."

Val took the basket and tried to remember where she'd seen eyes like that before. "Okay, but it sounds like I have to be careful about these special powers." She started reading the flavor labels. "Especially the habanero."

"Yeah, I'd stay away from that one. I made the mistake once of rubbing my eye while making a batch and thought I was going to have to call the fire department."

Val laughed. "You look really familiar," she said, but stopped short of adding that her unbelievably beautiful eyes were absolutely mesmerizing.

The woman took a moment to scrutinize her. She squinted her eyes slightly and said, "You're not from Hemlock…"

It was a little humorous that she knew Val wasn't a local. She'd already gotten that look a few times in the last twelve hours. "Not now, but I used to live here."

"What's your name?"

"Val Montague."

The woman smiled widely. "We went to high school together."

"We did?"

"I don't know if you remember me, but I'm Cam Nelson."

The eyes. It was in high school when she'd last seen them. "My God, yes! Wow."

"It's been a long time," Cam said.

"Twenty years."

"Never long enough."

Val remembered why. "People weren't that nice to you."

Cam chuckled, almost sadly. "No, they weren't."

They hadn't hung out together back then. Cam was from a very poor family whose father remained unemployed through high school. No matter what she did, she was never far from cruel remarks about her white-trash family. Whenever a break-in occurred at school or the students and teachers came back from the weekend to find something vandalized, Cam was the first person to be pulled to the principal's office.

Val didn't know if Cam was ever found guilty, but either way, it must have been hard to be instantly accused. She did act out often, and looking back, Val could understand that any teenager faced with constant blame and ridicule would do the same.

And Val had kept away from Cam, too. Unlike most of her friends, Val felt no desire to vilify her, but she'd kept her own distance from the conflict.

She also had to admit that she'd always been afraid of Cam Nelson. The girl with the intense eyes usually had an angry defiance that pervaded the halls like harsh perfume. Val wasn't sure what Cam would do if they ever accidentally bumped into each other in the halls so she stayed clear of her. Some students wouldn't leave her alone, though, harassing her as if they were fraternity idiots badgering a vulnerable homeless man just to get laughs.

Cam's parents weren't the highest models of society, and an abundance of stories were always circulating about their drinking and fighting, which invariably expanded into various rumors that, no matter how ridiculous, became the town's collective truth about the Nelsons.

"I can only imagine how tough it was in school."

"Back then, I was the kid of fucked-up parents. I hated it." Cam was scraping her fingernail on the counter as if trying to obliterate a spot. Or maybe a memory. "But even though they're gone, the town still has me to condemn."

"Still?"

"Big cities have sports teams or bad politicians to get all caught up in so they can have something to talk about and form opinions and be pissed at. Places like this have people like me."

"I'm sorry, Cam."

"Oh, I'm used to it now." She looked up from the counter. Her smile was beautiful, but Val felt so much sadness behind it. "And, hey, I get to make candy and eat as much as I want without getting in trouble."

Val laughed, though admittedly, it was more to break the uneasiness of the topic. "There's that, then. I always like to celebrate a fuck-you moment with a handful of saltwater taffy."

"You see? I told you my taffy was special."

Val liked her humor. She walked down the aisle, picking pieces to put in her basket and wondering how hard staying in Hemlock this whole time must have been on Cam.

When she reached the end of the first row, she glanced up and saw that Cam was looking her way. It seemed as if she were appraising her, and Val suddenly wondered if she'd aged well. Maybe she was getting a bit pudgier than she realized. Cam, on the other hand, looked terrific. She'd had one of the best bodies in high school, and to this day, it certainly hadn't betrayed her.

Val started down the next row and grabbed a few banana taffy pieces. Banana wasn't her favorite, but she was getting fidgety wondering what Cam thought of her. Then again, Cam probably wasn't thinking anything in particular. For all she knew she could be looking at the taffy bins and taking a mental inventory for refills.

Val was halfway down the row when Cam said, "I'm sorry about your mom."

"Thanks."

"Small town," she said, shrugging as if apologizing for knowing the gossip.

She looked up. "I'm sorry about your parents, too."

"Thanks. They've been gone for a while now."

"It sucks no matter when it happens."

"Yes, it does."

Cam left the counter area, and Val lost sight of her when she went to the back of the shop. When she returned, Cam had a tray of what looked like chocolate-covered pretzels.

She began to put them on the bottom shelf of the glass counter. "Are you just passing through?"

"Long enough to sell my mother's house."

"That's gotta be rough."

"Yeah." Val picked up a few strawberry taffy pieces and plunked them in her basket.

At the end of the row sat a cabinet that had solid wooden sides and a glass front. The shelves inside were fairly high up. Curious, she walked over and looked in. A display full of X-rated chocolate shapes surprised her. Virtually every male and female body part was available in both dark and milk chocolate. They were far out of the reach of young eyes, but she glanced back to the counter anyway.

Cam casually shrugged. "They sell well."

"I bet they're popular at bachelorette parties."

"They're just a sliver of that business. If you knew who came in here and bought those, your toes would curl."

"And these?" Val said as she walked over to a collection of T-shirts and coffee mugs. They were all emblazoned with a logo that read THE 45TH PARALLEL.

"They sell, too."

Val picked up a mug. “I feel sorry for those people who live on the 44th and 46th parallel.”

“Right? We might not be much, but they’re less than that.”

Cam amused her. She was witty and didn’t mind the small-town jokes. Val walked over to the counter and placed the mug and basket down on it.

“What can I say? People like a memento of a special place they’ve been to.”

Val smiled at her old classmate. “I’ll take all this candy and the mug, then.”

CHAPTER FOUR

Val spent the rest of the early afternoon driving around town, looking at what had changed, which was very little. Her mother's ashes rested in the box beside her, and every once in a while, Val talked out loud, commenting on something she saw, as if her mother were looking out the window, too.

When she returned to the house at two thirty, Nedra's car was gone. She retrieved the mail and went inside. When she put the candy and mug on the dining-room table, she saw a note resting there.

Val,

The open house went well. Quite a few people came through. I will let you know as soon as any call me about another look.

—Nedra.

Her phone rang so she put down the note. "Hello?"

"Valerie Montague?"

"Yes?"

"This is Max from American Insurance Fund. I wanted to let you know that we're sending out an adjuster to look at the car. He'll meet you at…

She could hear him shuffling through paperwork.

"...the Bob Mackinaw Garage at four o'clock tomorrow."

"Okay, thank you," she said as she sorted through the mail.

He gave her some other information as she carried the mail over to the couch. She was about to sit down when she noticed something strange. She quickly said good-bye to the agent and stared at the couch. One of the cushions has been turned sideways. She lifted it but found nothing underneath, so she put it back.

Its placement confused her. Why would someone want to mess with the couch? She set the mail down and slowly walked through the house to see if anything else was amiss.

At the entry of the kitchen, she scanned the room, but nothing seemed out of the ordinary. She opened the silverware drawer and inventoried the contents. Everything was there. The utility drawer was filled with rubber bands, pencils, thumbtacks, and other assorted things but otherwise looked ordinary. She closed the drawer and leaned against the counter. That cushion out of place was odd. Why would someone care about the couch?

Her mental exploration quickly fizzled out because she realized she was thirsty and a cold Diet Coke sounded really good. In the two steps it took to cross the kitchen, something on the floor flashed briefly. She knelt down and picked up two thumbtacks, just like the ones in the utility drawer. Now she was really perplexed. Her mother would have heard them drop, and no way would she have left them there.

Next, Val stood at the door of her mother's bedroom, much as she did the kitchen, and inspected the room. Again, everything seemed in order, but something was just a little off. She scanned the room a couple of times until she figured it out. The nightstand had been moved an inch to one side. The carpet impression, where the nightstand had been resting for years, showed to the right of where it now rested. She immediately checked her mother's jewelry case, the fear of a burglary making her pulse race, but thankfully everything was there.

Damn, she thought. After a check of the artwork around the house, her mother's electronics, and anything else she could remember, she decided nothing was missing.

Val got on the phone and called Nedra, telling her what she'd noticed.

"I watched everyone pretty closely. I'm sure nothing was taken, Val."

"It's just so strange. The couch cushion, the nightstand. This is a small town so I wouldn't expect—"

"Well, Hemlock has changed over the years. We have some very strange people here. The vagrants and ruffians who used to pass through are stopping here now and staying. Our crime rate has increased. My Lord, the Hemlock city council's talking about raising our taxes to hire more police officers." She sighed as if trying to calm herself down. "A lot of dangerous people are roaming the streets here now. They're just plain bad for business. But I can assure you, none of them came through your house today."

"I'm still confused as to why the couch cushion and nightstand were moved. And someone rummaged around in one of the kitchen drawers."

"People have their own ways of inspecting the houses they're looking to purchase."

"But the house is for sale, not the furniture."

"I know, dear. Even decent people have funny rituals. Please check that nothing was taken. If you see anything gone, please call me right away. We're bonded and insured."

"Well, nothing's gone as far as I can tell."

"You just let me know. And I'll tell any other agents that show your home that they are to stay with their clients at all times."

Before hanging up, she thanked Nedra but was still baffled.

Rather than go to the store and buy food to make dinner, Val decided to go out to eat. Her stomach had growled its loud dissatisfaction that all she'd had that day was some taffy.

The town had one fast-food place and three small restaurants that mostly catered to the summer's seasonal crowd. Two of the sit-down establishments served seafood, but Val wasn't in the mood for that so she went to see if the 45th Parallel Pantry was still in business.

The building was, but the name of the place was now the Halfway Cafe. The different paint scheme and new sign meant it had probably changed hands, but she decided to try it out anyway.

The inside was still very simple, but it was now decorated in a man-cave kind of theme. Its brown and white walls sported neon beer signs and pictures of athletes and macho movie stars.

Ten or so people sat at tables. It didn't have a bar or TVs, which made it a little more obvious that the place was a local hangout. As she looked for an open table, she scanned the room. A woman looked her way, and when her gaze lingered, Val studied her face.

She seemed to be Val's age. She looked familiar except Val didn't know anyone who wore leather pants and a biker jacket. As she studied her, the woman suddenly jumped up from her chair and headed right for her.

"Val!"

It was the voice that roused Val's memory. "Donna?"

After they hugged, Donna said, "Damn, it's been years." She paused a moment and said, "I'm so sorry about your mom."

"Yeah." Was she going to have this conversation with virtually everyone in Hemlock?

"It's so good to see you, Val." She touched her arm. "Come sit with us."

Donna led her back to the table and introduced her to a man named Buzz, who looked like he'd gotten off the same motorcycle as Donna.

"Are you hungry?" Donna said as the waitress delivered a check.

"You've already eaten."

"It's okay. Go ahead and order."

Val asked the waitress for a cheeseburger and a Diet Coke.

"Best food in Hemlock," Donna said, "but that's not saying much."

Buzz reached into his pocket and pulled out a billfold.

"I'm gonna stay a while," Donna told him.

He placed some money on top of the check and nodded to Val. "Nice to meet you," he said, and walked out of the restaurant.

Donna drank from her beer. "Damn, woman. It's been years!"

"About twenty, hasn't it?"

"Yeah, I guess it has. You left right after high-school graduation. Couldn't wait to get out of here."

"What's with the biker clothes? I remember a sunny little cheerleader."

"I'm not that sunny anymore."

Silence crept in and they both looked down at the table.

Val was just about to ask her who Buzz was when Donna spoke first. "I've missed you all these years."

"We had some great times, didn't we?"

"Yes. And I always wondered why you left so fast."

Val shrugged. The reaction felt as feeble as it must have looked. "I just wanted to get away."

Donna hesitated. "So it wasn't…me? Us?"

"It was a lot of things, I guess."

Donna tapped her fingers on the beer mug. The movement could have suggested frustration or resentment, but when Val saw her bite her lip, she knew it was something else. She reached over and placed her hand on Donna's.

"You haven't thought all these years…"

Donna shrugged, and Val realized she'd carried it longer than Val had.

"Well, the last thing I knew, we were…close, and then you took off for Texas or somewhere."

"You were my best buddy, Donna." Val stopped and corrected herself. "More than that. And it was great. I just couldn't…"

"Be with me?"

"Stay."

"You did have a shitty home life. I'm sorry you did. And if any part of your leaving was because of us, I'm sorry."

"To be honest, some of it was. It was hard to be with you and watch you date guys."

"You know why."

"Yes. Our parents would have killed us both," Val said. "But I just couldn't stay here. Plus, I didn't think my lifestyle would stick with you."

"It did. Kind of. I guess I can say that I have twice the chance of getting a date."

Val smiled and shook her head.

"Is that your husband?"

"Buzz?" Donna jerked her head toward the door he'd just walked through. "No, he's a friend. But he also doesn't need to hear anything that isn't his business. People talk, you know."

"What about you? Are you seeing anyone?"

"Not right now."

"Still like women?" Donna seemed almost shy about asking, which contradicted her kick-ass, leather look.

"Yes. Always have."

Swirling her beer, Donna said, "You were just really special to me, you know? I mean, I know it was a long time ago, but we had something great, didn't we?"

"We did. My first."

Donna gazed at her and seemed to be recalling a specific memory.

"What?" Val said.

"Nothing. I'm just glad to see you. Hell, I know we've all moved on. It's just when your mom died, I knew you'd be coming back to town and that brought it all back."

Donna smiled at Val, and the traumas of youth seemed to have settled down.

Val pointed a finger at her. "No harm?"

Donna pointed one back. "No foul."

Together they said, "No blood, no ambulance!"

They laughed and a few people close by stared at them. The waitress brought Val's cheeseburger and drink.

"Ah," Val said, "women's basketball was great, wasn't it?"

"Yeah. The after-game parties were even better."

Val regarded Donna, wondering how much her departure had hurt her. She said her next words gently. "Shall we chalk up our time back then as the joys of 'experimental youth'?"

Donna smiled. "Yes. And then some."

She raised her Diet Coke. "I'll drink to that."

After they clinked glasses, Donna said, "How are you doing?"

"Things are okay. I just picked up my mom's ashes. She has instructions on where to scatter them. It's pretty surreal, you know?"

"It must be. I'm so sorry."

"I figure I'll go do that tomorrow. Then I have to stop by Mack's garage in the afternoon."

"Why Mack's?"

"I had an accident last night."

"What happened?"

"Oh, I hit a damn deer. Well, someone else hit it and then it flew into my car."

"Are you okay?"

"We weren't hurt, but the deer didn't make it."

"They usually don't," Donna said. "How long are you in town?"

"I'm not sure. I need to pack her things and get the house sold."

"Nedra's handling it."

"How'd you know?"

Donna looked at Val and blinked once. "Nedra owns this town's real-estate racket."

Val nodded, falling silent. It was all so much to deal with. Her brain felt more tired than her body had ever experienced. Her sorrow about losing her mother was hitting her harder than she'd expected. She'd known that coming back to Hemlock would bring up emotions. She just hadn't planned for them to feel like cinder blocks.

Donna nudged her arm. "Hey. You up for a movie tomorrow night?"

"I think so."

"It'll help you get your mind off things."

"Is there still only one choice?"

Donna laughed. "Yup. The Bijou. One showing. Eight thirty. This town is still a one-trick pony."

CHAPTER FIVE

The dreams that plagued Val all night were bizarre—sleep-stealing, short bursts of a cacophony of images that jumbled together. In one, forests slid down mountains and cars crashed in endless succession. In another, it seemed like every face of every person in town took turns pushing right up to Val, shoving exaggerated, toothless smiles and gawking stares in her face and cackling like deranged carnival barkers from an evil circus. And the last one, with her tied to her old high-school English desk while the place was totally engulfed in fire, and a school assembly, with everyone but her safely out on the front lawn, unable to hear her screaming, jarred her awake and forced her to get up just to end the demented menagerie.

Her second day in town wasn't starting out any better than her first. With a crashed car that needed to get fixed, she first had to fulfill her mother's wishes.

About twenty miles south of town, the Coast Highway traveled through less-populated areas. Marshland to the right and the coastal mountains to the left provided a beautiful corridor for her drive.

But her heart hung in her chest, feeling like a wrecking ball dangling from a construction crane. Inert and lifeless, it seemed to be suspended, waiting there for something, or perhaps someone, to persuade it to move, to beat, just a little.

She approached and passed a green highway sign she hadn't thought about since she left after high school. Slowing the car down, she pulled off on a diminutive patch of gravel that served as the parking lot for the Cape Foulweather overlook.

She got out of the car, assuming that her mother in the box on her seat wouldn't mind a quick stopover. The state beach sign was still there, though the wood was wind-worn in places. She could still read about Captain James Cook and how, in March of 1778, he spotted this small but intimidating promontory, made from the solid basalt of an ancient volcano, and gave it its name.

And it was true that the five-hundred-foot-high, oversized rock would receive the worst of the ocean's temper, with unannounced bashing rain and one-hundred-mile-an-hour winds more common than not. Accidents along this stretch of the highway occurred frequently, as well, to the unsuspecting drivers who failed to anticipate the instant weather changes that swept through this small stretch.

This is where Mother Nature and the Greek god of the sea, Poseidon, conspired together to create a place where mortals would be constantly reminded of the power of both. Its inimitable combination of rock and sea fused like two warring factions. But here, she'd always thought, they had joined forces to declare their immeasurable force. It was both amazing and sobering.

Hiking out to the cliff's edge, she realized the view hadn't changed at all. The vast expanse of the ocean was much more obvious from that vantage point, and a visitor could spot incoming swells long before reaching the rocky shoreline below. Otter Rock and the Devil's Punch Bowl were visible in the south, and on fogless days, one could even make out the community of Yaquina Head. She peered out over the water and watched the activity on Gull Rock, a small, domed island almost due west of her. Small dots of seagulls took off and landed with the tempo of shoppers in and out of a busy grocery store. The dark hump, rising only eight or ten feet above the water, seemed to be a shared rest stop of sorts, giving the birds a quick respite between their never-ending search for unsuspecting fish rising too close to the surface of the wide expanses of the Pacific Ocean.

Val stepped closer to the edge and took in a deep breath. She closed her eyes to amplify her sense of hearing. She recognized the squawking of a group of seagulls below but listened for the sound she liked the most. She didn't have to wait long, for a swell had come in and there it was—the quick, almost imperceptible smacking of the water on the rocks just before the more noticeable crashing sound of the wave as it broke apart. It was like a one-two punch, minute after minute, year after year. That smack before the crash, as if the ocean were trying to literally break the rocks. And the rocks stood fast and firm, simply waiting for the water to dissipate. But in reality, each initial smack did damage the rocks, if only knocking off a millionth of a millimeter from its exterior. And while the mass of the rocks outwardly seemed to win each barrage, time was on the side of the persistence of the sea, eventually wearing down its foe, over millennia, winning the war, even if the human eye couldn't witness it.

Val opened her eyes. She felt kin to the rocks. She wasn't strong and determined enough to win at much of anything. Her last relationship had failed miserably, and she knew her own contribution to its collapse was her inability to retain the fortitude to fight for it. The ex, who now lived in Val's house in Dallas while she had to rent a condo, was like the ocean, smacking away at her with snipes and barbs throughout the relationship because Val wasn't home enough or didn't listen enough. Those little jabs had worn away at her until she'd simply left. They were together three years, but it hadn't taken a millennium for Val to crumble. More like the last two of those years.

She wasn't good at conflict. It wasn't lost on her that she'd left Hemlock as soon as she was old enough to drive. Granted, her mother's boyfriends held an absolutely unequaled power over her, especially when her mom sided with them, but even in her adulthood, she was never the ocean. Always the slow, crumbling rock.

She looked strong, even acted strong, but clashes were always her undoing.

Gusts of wind whipped up and over the cliff a little more robustly now, pushing at her as if Poseidon himself were warning her to stand back. She thought of the rocks below her receiving the brunt of his force and realized quickly that she was in no position to engage in any resistance.

She took one last look at Gull Rock and wondered if the gulls ever felt as tiny as she did right then.

Driving down off Cape Foulweather, she knew it was only another few miles to the Siletz River turnoff.

Val opened the note again and read the directions. It told her to drive past the city of Siletz, which was approximately eight miles inland from the ocean.

She put the note back on the passenger's seat next to her mother's cremains box and focused on the small, winding road.

The river ambled along to her right, never widening farther than one hundred feet and mostly spanning fifty or less. It was mostly brackish closer to the sea, and opportunistic, reddish-brown sea lions often traveled up its narrow channels, looking for rockfish and salmon, deciding sometimes to stay upriver for days.

Val's schooling had taught her which tree was which so she could point out the differences between Sitka spruces and Western hemlocks like they were independent but analogous fraternal twins. And the abundance of the trees was always so magnificent in Oregon. The need for auto deodorizers was nonexistent because all one had to do was roll down the windows and the freshest pine aromas would bathe the car for free.

Val passed Cedar Creek Drift and Euchre Creek, slowing down to pass over the Second Steel Bridge and into the town of Siletz. On any other day, she would have stopped and wandered around the quaint little fishing town, but she had a mission.

When she reached the town of Logsden, she passed through it as well and slowed to read the note again. It said to cross a bridge and turn left onto Moonshine Park Road. She followed it for about four miles and after the left turn passed underneath the gateway sign of Moonshine Park.

She didn't remember ever being here. Maybe her mother had taken her, but if she did, the place must have changed over the years because she didn't recognize any of it. She parked, picked up the box, and got out of the car.

The area was quite beautiful and very secluded. Tent and camping sites with fire rings and picnic tables were all located close to the edge of the Siletz. Only a few of them were being used, which was logical since it was already winter.

The note said to walk up the river, past the group-camping and larger RV sites, and to look for a drift-boat launch. She found it after walking for a few minutes. By now, no other people were around, and Val was glad for that. She really didn't want anyone watching her. It wasn't that she was afraid the releasing of cremains was illegal. She actually had no idea if it was or not, but she wanted to be alone.

The last line on the note read, *Look for a maintained trail on an abandoned spur road and choose a nice place.*

That was the end of the instructions. The rest, she guessed, was up to her.

The trail she came upon hadn't really been maintained, but it was the only one she found so she hiked down it, following it as it meandered away from the river and then rejoined its banks. She decided to stop by a group of Sitka spruce trees. They were the much-more dwarfed cousins of their superlative Canadian relatives, whose tops could reach three hundred feet, but these conifers were just as beautiful. These old girls stood proud, showing off their stiff, sharp needles and graceful buff-brown cylindrical cones, knowing that the makers of violins and the builders of sailing boats revered their knotless bodies for their unique strength-to-weight ratio. But Val liked them for their uplifting elegance. And she was certain her mother would, too.

She knelt and placed the box at the base of the closest tree. Pausing for a moment, she looked around just to make sure this was the right place. She supposed it didn't matter in the long run. Her mother would return to the earth, and eventually wind and rain would meld her existence with the rest of what God created until she was no more, or maybe all, of this area.

She opened the box and pulled out a large plastic bag. Setting it in front of her knees, she examined it as if she might recognize something. It was silly, she knew, but this was her mother. Or had been.

The ashes were made up of mostly dust, but as she poked at the bag a little, she could see small bits of what? Bone?

And then she began to sob. The finality of what she was looking at struck her like a slap of thunder. She cried for her mom and for herself, not caring that the tears flowed so hard she couldn't see the bag below her or the trees right next to her.

She felt as tiny as the smallest pebble, whose individual significance meant next to nothing. She was five years old again, in that house back in Hemlock, crying for her mom to hold her because of a bad dream. She needed her again and she was gone. This was what finality was and what a broken heart truly felt like.

Val's nose began to run, mixing with the cascade of tears, and she knelt there and wailed for a long time.

At some point, a slight wind chilled the wetness on her cheeks and her crying subsided. She inhaled deeply through her mouth since her nose had plugged up long before. She wiped her face with the back of her sleeve and blinked until she could see a little clearer.

She looked up at the spruce trees that had been waiting patiently for her to get it all out. They were so matronly and resilient, confirming with such resolute deportment that they were up for the job of accepting and watching over the ashes. Val now was doubly sure this was the right place for her mom.

When she could see the plastic bag again, she took off the twist tie. A wisp of the lightest of her mom's ashes floated up like an ethereal cloud escaping the rest. Val wasn't sure if she should follow a certain procedure or method for scattering ashes, so she supported the bottom of the bag with one hand and tilted it with the other. As some of the ashes began to fall, she stopped.

Should she say something? She knew the 23rd Psalm, but was that appropriate?

"Fuck all," she said, and bowed her head.

"Mom, I wish you well and I wish for you the freedom in death that you never had in life. May these trees and the beauty of this forest and river protect you, and may you have an everlasting smile because you are now at peace."

Slowly, she lifted the bag and started pouring the ashes out. She got up from her knees and walked around to the other trees as the cremains both fell to the ground and were picked up by the wind.

Her mother was now everywhere, in wisps of whitish-gray, settling on the pine needles and coming to rest around the trunks. Part of her blew into the river and disappeared under the water.

When the bag was empty, Val remained there, watching the wind, which still had some moving around to do. Her mother didn't completely settle for many more minutes, and when she did, Val stayed even longer. Her mind was wholly and utterly blank. She felt the breezes around her and the softness of the pine-needled ground. A hawk screeched somewhere above her, and the grasses along the bank rustled.

She listened to the song that nature was performing, knowing that nothing else at that very moment was more important.

Finally, she blinked and slowly came back. She noticed the bag in her hand and the car keys that had shifted in her pocket and were now rather uncomfortable. Her head hurt, and she was aware of the puffiness around the edges of her eyes.

She took one last look at the trees.

"Thank you," she told them and began her walk, back the way she'd come.

CHAPTER SIX

Val sat in the waiting room of Mack's garage. It was a bit past four o'clock, and she'd had a few hours to collect herself. She'd stopped off at a diner to wash her face in the bathroom and order an iced tea. Her eyes still felt puffy, but she really didn't care.

She waited for the insurance agent and hoped he wouldn't be too late. The place was fairly busy, for such a small town, but being one of only two garages within a half an hour's drive, maybe this was normal.

All the chairs in the waiting room were filled. Two mothers were monitoring two children each, and a man was reading a magazine. The four kids surrounded the drink dispenser that was filled with bright-pink liquid. They hovered around it taking turns, filling paper cups and drinking noisily.

One of the mothers calmly called out to her child. "Sam, that'll be your fourth cup. Don't you think you've had enough?"

He finished one last gulp, which ended in a very loud *ahhh*. "I think I've got room for one more."

One of the little girls drained the last of her cup and went over to the other mother, speaking a whole sentence in just one word. "MommmIgottago."

The mothers exchanged knowing smirks, and the one that belonged to the girl began to stand. "Let's go—"

The child darted out the door to the garage. "Icandoitmyself!"

Amused, Val watched the mother sit back down, probably getting used to this new independence.

She looked toward the garage and saw that Mack was still busy talking to another customer. She scrutinized the lemonade dispenser. Its cold, pink liquid was certainly inviting. As she got up and walked over to it, she maneuvered between the kids and said, "Don't tell Mack." The mothers watched their kids laugh at the adult lady who helped herself to a cup.

She enjoyed how cool and refreshing it tasted. And just as she tilted the last of it back, Mack boomed through the door and into the waiting room. Val jumped and then froze, cup in hand. Mack asked one of the mothers to accompany him out to her car so he could explain something.

Just then, the little girl came bounding back from the bathroom and to the lemonade dispenser. Val decided to quit while she was ahead of a Mack scolding and sat back down. She checked her watch. It was a quarter after four.

She decided that she'd use the restroom, wait another ten minutes, and then call the agent.

Walking through the garage, she found the bathroom off to the side and entered.

As she closed the door and turned on the light, she heard a whirring sound. She looked for the source of the noise but figured it was coming from some pneumatic tool or something out in the garage. There was one toilet and a sink, and by the way these two very old and tired-looking pieces leaned away from each other, it looked as if they'd been unhappily married for fifty years.

She sat down on the toilet and heard the high-pitched *zizzing* of a compressed-air gun. After she listened to a few more clangs and thuds, she surmised that the bathroom door must have been made of material no thicker than cardboard. Peeing in the melodic ambiance of a mechanic's garage wasn't the most peaceful experience, but it would certainly drown out all noise from inside the bathroom.

She washed her hands and opened the door. The whirring sound suddenly stopped.

"Good timing," she thought to herself as another child, evidently full of lemonade, pushed his way past her.

Val stepped back into the waiting room as a man in khakis and a golf shirt entered. He looked around and guessed that Val was his client because he approached her first.

"Valerie Montague?"

"Val, yes."

"I'm Bill Perkins from American Insurance Fund. I'm here to look at the damage on the car."

Mack returned with the mother, so Val got his attention and introduced him to Bill. They shook hands quickly.

"I won't be long," Bill said. "I just need to take some pictures of the car."

They followed Mack to the last repair bay.

Bill made a little noise that could have been mistaken for an aborted hiccup. "The hood's been taken off."

Mack looked too busy to care. "Yup."

"You've already started fixing the car."

"Had to. Cars are lining up left and right. The hood's laying out back."

"We're supposed to have pictures of the car before any repairs begin. It's much more difficult to determine what damage was due to the accident directly and what might have been damaged prior. Or after."

Mack stood there as if he was waiting for the adjuster to continue talking, hardly moved by anything he'd just said.

Finally, Mr. Perkins said, "May I see the hood?"

They followed Mack through a door that opened up to a shed filled with car parts of all types. Val's hood lay on a heap of junk in one corner. It was pretty banged up. The adjuster stepped closer and inspected it. He looked at Mack, pointing out a few hammer marks and fresh creases.

Mack was picking something out of his teeth. "It was a bitch getting it off."

The adjuster shook his head and silently snapped some photographs. Turning to Mack he said, "I'll need a few of the car, as well."

❖

Val pushed a shopping cart toward a checkout stand. She'd decided she should probably get some groceries for the house after all. She couldn't eat every meal at the Halfway Cafe.

The grocery store was fairly busy. Standing in line, she listened to the activities around her—the *blip*, *blip* of items being scanned, the elevator music playing overhead, and the hum of the refrigerated grab-and-go soda case next to her.

It took her a moment to register what was going on in front of her. The woman checking out looked fairly normal, but the items she was buying certainly weren't. The checker didn't seem to be as interested as Val as she scanned KY jelly, rubber gloves, baby powder, and a rope.

Val was so engrossed in what she was watching that she jumped when a hand squeezed her shoulder. She turned to see Cam, who was holding a basket of groceries.

"I'm sorry, did I scare you?"

Val shook her head but said, "Yeah, a little. I was just…"

"Marveling at the price of rubber gloves?" Cam whispered.

"Yes! That's it!" She relaxed and was grateful she didn't have to explain her interest in the strange items the checker was now bagging.

She hadn't realized how happy she'd be to see Cam again and was glad she'd chosen to go to the store when she had.

"How are you?" Cam asked.

Val stepped forward and started unloading her things. "Low on supplies."

Cam looked over Val's groceries and saw a Hershey bar on the belt. "Chocolate, too?"

"Sometimes a girl's just gotta have her chocolate. What am I saying? You're the expert on that. Am I right?"

Cam smiled. "You're correct. And today just happens to be my turtle-making day. Why don't you come by and I'll make you some special ones. They'll be nice and warm."

"That sounds too heavenly to turn down."

"Good." Cam's wide smile looked cute on her. "Around six?"

Val grabbed the Hershey bar and put it back on the candy rack next to her. "If I'm early, don't hold it against me."

Cam laughed and said good-bye as she walked away to finish her shopping.

Val watched her for a moment. She sure was beautiful, she thought. Dealing with a dead mother certainly wasn't the best circumstance under which to meet someone as wonderful as Cam, but the little flutter in her heart told her not to sweat it. And she really wanted to go by the candy store for some fresh turtles.

❖

It didn't take long to return to her mother's house and drop off the groceries. She brought the mail in and cleaned the coffeemaker before changing into some more comfortable jeans and a lightweight red sweater. She grabbed her mom's house keys again and left.

When Val walked into Cam's candy shop, the aroma of chocolate was twice as strong as before. Cam stood bent over a cauldron, and when Val got closer, she could see that Cam's rubber-gloved hands were covered in thick brown liquid heaven.

"Wow," she said.

Cam slowly pulled her hand out of the chocolate she'd been stirring. "I like to feel the consistency. It's weird, but it works for me."

"Hey, who am I to judge what a woman does with her chocolate?"

Cam placed a glob of it on a graham cracker and handed it to her. "Here."

"This looks incredible."

"It should tide you over until the turtles are finished."

Val took the graham cracker and sat on a stool close to Cam. Taking a bite, she closed her eyes and groaned. "I think the Virgin Mary just blessed me."

Cam looked at her with those penetrating slate-blue eyes, and a hot tremor ran through her. She stopped mid-chew, not sure of what to do or say next. Ripples of desire crept up her back, and her sudden desire for this woman surprised her. Not that Cam wasn't magnificent; it was just that she'd barely met her. Yet, her body was acting on its own, shuddering so deeply, with no care about how obvious it must have made her look.

The corner of Cam's mouth curled up into a half smile.

Val wanted to kiss her. She could easily lean over and—

Cam spoke suddenly. "That's about the best compliment I've ever gotten."

The suggestive moment passed. It was obviously a one-sided moment, and Val secretly admonished herself. She relaxed a little but was honestly disappointed. "It's true."

"I haven't even added the caramel and nuts."

"That says a lot, then. If the chocolate is this good, it'll only be better with the added ingredients. It's like pancake batter."

"Pancake batter?"

Val nodded as she licked her fingers. "Taste pancake batter before it goes onto the skillet. If it tastes bland or chalky, the pancakes will just be okay. But add sugar and cinnamon until the batter tastes really good. Bam, killer pancakes."

"Makes sense."

"Of course, I know nothing about dessert making. That's a particularly involved science. All I know is your chocolate is amazing."

"Only the finest. And I'm proud to declare that this establishment is carob-free."

"Thank God. I hate carob."

"It was invented for people who can't handle happiness."

Val laughed. "But how can you stand to be here all day with this yummy-smelling candy practically screaming at you?"

Cam put on a new pair of gloves. "Oh, it's worse than that." She gestured upward. "I live over the store."

"You've either gone stark raving mad or you've become immune to the aroma."

"I can't verify for sure that I'm not crazy, but I am immune to the lure of chocolate. And it's probably for the better. I'd weigh four hundred pounds if I let myself go in here."

Val watched Cam lean over the chocolate and stared at the muscles in her back. Cam had to work out, because simply stirring liquids sure hadn't shaped that kind of body.

"I somehow doubt you'd let yourself go like that," Val said, suddenly wondering why she'd said that out loud.

Though Cam smiled, Val couldn't tell how she'd taken the comment and privately yelled at herself for her ill-mannered conduct.

"So, I've already lightly toasted the whole pecans," Cam said as she moved a large cookie sheet over to the marble-topped prep table.

Cam had changed the subject. Slightly embarrassed, Val decided to just concentrate on the task at hand, focusing on the metal sheets holding marvelous lumps of something that looked ready to eat just as they were.

"And earlier," Cam said, "I coated each cluster of pecans, here, with homemade caramel. That kind of acts like glue to keep the nuts together."

"The pecans are shaped like real turtles with legs and a head. Usually, I see them as just huge, round hunks."

Cam chuckled. "A lot of places believe in super-size marketing. I never wanted to do that."

"Kind of like a less-is-more belief."

"Precisely. So, the caramel has set and now it's time for the chocolate."

"Awesome."

Cam stared at her, and Val quickly looked around the room as if she'd knocked something over. Maybe she had chocolate on her face. She swiped her mouth. When Cam still stared, Val spoke. "What?"

"You don't think I'm going to do this all by myself, do you?"

Val jumped off the stool. "I can help?"

Her answer was the pair of gloves and a large spoon Cam handed her.

"You fill the spoon," she said when Val was ready, "and then pour it over the first pecan cluster."

With her own spoon, Val followed what Cam was doing. When they'd finished the sixteen turtles on the sheet, Val was as blissful as Rembrandt must have been after completing a portrait.

"That's all there is to it?" Val wanted to lick the spoon.

"That's all, except we have about twenty more sheets to finish."

"May I help with those, too?"

"I was hoping you would."

As they stood side by side spooning chocolate, they talked about high school and which classmates still lived in Hemlock. Val laughed when Cam told her she would have liked to think it was kismet that found them in the same grocery store at the same time, but with only one store in town, it was more like a high-probability equation.

"Well, we could have missed each other by minutes."

"That's true," Cam said as she moved two sheets to a cooling rack and brought two more over. "So tell me more about the accident. The deer hit a woman's car and then flew over and hit yours?

"Yeah. Scared the hell out of me."

"Wow."

Val spooned a little too much on one turtle. "Shoot. This one got messed up."

"Not to worry," Cam said. "I sell them by weight and can guarantee you that someone will always ask for the fattest one."

Val went back to spooning. "I feel bad for the poor deer. They're such beautiful animals."

"Where's your car now?"

"At Mack's garage."

Cam nodded, but Val noticed her face change. Her lip tightened and her nod was brusque.

"You don't like him?"

"He was with my ex, that's all. It was years ago, but they started sleeping together before we broke up."

"I didn't know Mack was gay."

Cam's eyebrows rose when she looked at her. Val smiled her best goofy clown face, and Cam broke into a laugh.

"For a minute there, I thought you were clueless."

Val turned to dip out another scoop of chocolate. "I am about a lot of things. But I'm glad I wasn't about you."

When she looked up, Cam's spoon was coming her way, and it landed with a plunk on her nose.

"I'm glad you're glad," Cam said. Her expression was so warm and considerate, and Val couldn't remember connecting with someone this quickly and this easily.

"Anyway," Cam said, "it's water long gone under the bridge now. We broke up a while ago, and I'm just not on speaking terms with either of them now."

Val wiped the chocolate off her nose. "Thank God there's another mechanic in town, too."

"You're right about that one." Cam spooned some more chocolate onto a clump of pecans. "How badly was the other woman hurt by the deer?"

"She wasn't."

Cam seemed to contemplate the statement before saying, "A deer hits her car and she's not hurt? How's her car?"

"Damaged."

"Totaled?"

Val shook her head. "Front-end damage. Grill, hood. Hers was drivable."

Cam frowned. "Every car I've ever seen that's hit a deer is pretty much totaled." She shrugged. "Strange things happen, I guess."

"Well, that was my first deer. And I hope it's my last."

Cam smiled again. "I hope you weren't too uncomfortable with that dead deer riding in the back of Mack's tow truck."

"The deer?"

"Didn't Mack come out and tow you back?"

"Yes, but he didn't get the deer."

When Cam frowned again, Val said, "What?"

"Mack's one of the biggest hunters around. He'd never miss out on venison, whether he bagged it or not. Was the deer too far destroyed?"

"I don't think so. It was in the forest just off the road. I was planning to go see if it was still alive, but the girl in the other car told me not to."

"And Mack didn't even go look at it?"

"No."

"I'd call that an unexpected turn."

"The whole event was unexpected."

They finished the last of the sheets of turtles, and Val was unusually disappointed that she had to leave. "I hate to go, but I've got plans tonight. I want you to know, though, that I had a really wonderful time today."

"I'm glad. I did, too." Cam filled a small bag with turtles and handed it to Val. "I pay my help in sugar, corn syrup, and nuts."

"This is so awesome! I'm quitting my job back home. Those bastards pay me with very untasty pieces of paper."

As Val stepped toward the door, Cam touched her arm. "I'm not sure how long you're going to be in town, but will you come by again?"

A lightness filled Val's chest and she welcomed the feeling. "If there weren't a drop of chocolate or taffy in this place, I would still most definitely come back."

Cam's smile couldn't have felt better to Val. She wanted to run as fast as she could to her car. She resisted, but it was very difficult.

❖

After two decades, the Bijou was still open for business. It still had only one movie per night, and it always started at the same time. The marquee outside advertised the night's offering, which changed every other Friday, and because the theater was located on the main road through town, the owner never advertised anywhere else. People just knew.

Val found Donna waiting in the lobby, where they bought popcorn and drinks before finding seats. The theater was filling up well for a Wednesday.

Donna was catching Val up on her new job as an office secretary in Newport when Val stopped her.

"That woman," she said, tapping Donna on the arm, "That's the one I was in the accident with. I mean it was her car that the deer hit first."

"Really?"

She looked even younger than she did that rainy night. She was dressed and made up like a thirteen-year-old. Val watched her locate who she was looking for and take a seat next to him. The man was close to sixty years old and seemed very happy to see her.

"I don't think that's her father," Val said.

"To each his own, I suppose."

The lights dimmed and the first movie trailer started. Val couldn't help but take another look at the woman and didn't like that she was now making out with the old guy.

She stuffed a handful of popcorn into her mouth and wondered if that little dalliance would become the next bit of fodder for the gossip-hungry townsfolk.

❖

Val woke up suddenly. The house was quiet, and she couldn't remember hearing anything that might have woken her. She threw the covers off to sit up, but she paused. Her head swam as if she'd been drinking way too much alcohol, but all she'd consumed was a Diet Coke and popcorn.

Startled, she dropped her head and stared at her sweats and T-shirt, waiting for the wooziness to subside. Nausea gripped her stomach, and when she tried to stand, she pitched forward and fell to the floor. She was able to reach up and turn the nightstand lamp on, but a shock of dizziness slammed into her head and she crumpled to the floor.

Something was terribly wrong. She held her head and groaned out loud. Sick and confused, she reached for her cell phone and dialed 911. As the operator answered, she tried to speak, but everything went black.

❖

When Val opened her strangely heavy eyelids, she realized she was in a bed, propped up by pillows. An oxygen tube was taped just under her nose, and a pink, plastic, kidney-shaped dish lay next to her hand. She was somehow wearing a light-blue cotton gown with little gold diamonds on it.

She heard some scuffling noises before what looked like a doctor and nurse entered from around a curtain and walked over to her bedside. "How are you feeling?"

Compared to what, Val thought. It was hard to engage her brain in any kind of recall. "A little nauseous. What happened?"

"You were found unconscious in your house. When the police arrived, they smelled natural gas. You must have been exposed to it long enough to become fairly sick."

Val vaguely remembered waking up and trying to get to her phone, but that was about it.

"Your blood looks good, and if your symptoms don't get any worse in the next hour or so, you should be able to be released. Of course, you won't be able to stay in your house until the gas department fixes the leak."

The doctor opened a chart and began writing in it while the nurse poured her some water. She handed her the cup, along with some aspirin.

"Take this," she said.

Her head pounded with the fervor of an entire crew of overly busy house roofers.

As she drank, the nurse said, "We called your friend Donna. She said she'd come by to pick you up."

"Thank you." She handed the cup back. "Do you know if the house is okay?"

"The paramedics that brought you in told me that a police officer turned off the gas main. I doubt the gas company will be out tonight. You'll be able to go home after they confirm that your house is safe to re-enter. Now just relax for a while and we'll check in on you later."

They left, and Val lay there wondering how long the gas had been leaking. She hadn't smelled anything when she'd gotten home from the movies.

She drifted off in a sort of hazy nap. She could hear people talking outside her door and intercoms calling for doctors. She dozed off and on, and the short moments of light slumber were filled with images of her mom, the highway into Hemlock, and Donna and Cam. Part of the movie they'd seen flashed in her head as well. All were just rapid, random clips whose fleeting emergence startled her awake each time.

At some point, she awoke to the doctor asking, "Any more nausea?"

"No." She blinked at the light he'd turned on. "I'm feeling better."

"That's good. You'll probably have a headache tomorrow, but it's nothing that some aspirin won't help. There's no need to take anything stronger. I just want you to be aware of any other symptoms. Breathing problems, nausea, continued headaches, anything that concerns you."

The bedside curtain ruffled and Donna appeared.

"My Lord! Are you okay?"

The doctor wrote some things down and left.

"Yeah," she said to Donna, who took a seat in the chair next to her bed.

"Gas leaks scare the hell out of me. Can you imagine what would have happened if you hadn't woken up?"

Val looked sideways at Donna.

"Shit." Donna shook her head. "That was dumb to say."

"It's okay."

"Are they going to release you tonight?"

"Yeah, in a little while."

"Well, it'll be a tight squeeze at my apartment. It's a one-bedroom, and I've got four friends staying there from out of town, but we'll figure something out."

"That's okay. I can stay at a motel."

"I won't have it! Maybe I can get some of them to stay somewhere else."

"No, there's no reason. I'll get a room."

Donna looked at her, lips tight in disapproval.

"Really! I'd rather. I could use the peace and quiet of a motel room. Could you just take me back to my car?"

"What if you get sick again?"

"I'll call you."

"You've always had a mind of your own, haven't you?"

"Yes. And thanks for coming to get me."

❖

When Donna pulled up to the Montague house, Val could see a piece of paper taped to the front door. They got out, walked up, and read the note.

DANGER! GAS LEAK—FUMES PRESENT. DO NOT ENTER UNTIL CLEARED BY OREGON GAS DEPARTMENT.

Something was handwritten below it.

Val read it out loud.

Gas Dept. contacted. They will come by tomorrow between 10 and 2. HPD

Val tapped on the note and turned to Donna, who stepped up and leaned around her to look at the note.

"This is a special invitation to any burglars who want to come rob me."

"No one's gonna go inside with those fumes," Donna said. "And if they do, you'll probably find them passed out on the floor like you were."

"Say, do you suppose they really mean not to enter or just don't enter and stay?"

"What?"

"I need to go inside and get my shoes."

"Are you nuts?"

"I'm still in my damn socks, Donna."

"I'll go get you a pair of my shoes."

"It'll just take a minute."

"Val! There are gas fumes in there! They sent you to the hospital!"

She ignored Donna's protests and opened the door. She put her upper arm to her face, using her T-shirt sleeve as a mask, and ran inside.

She held her breath while she darted into her room and grabbed some shoes and a bra. Luckily, the police had taken her car keys, phone, and wallet to the hospital and dropped them off. She snatched the manila envelope from the table and then paused. She looked around for anything else she might need, but quickly realized that air was more important than anything else so she dashed back outside.

"See?" Val took a deep breath, "No sweat."

Donna didn't look pleased at all. "Did you get dropped on your head when you were a baby?"

"Funny," Val said, and took a step toward the garage to get her rental car. She began to wobble and bent over.

Donna was right there, steadying her by the arm.

"No driving for you. You're coming to my place."

Val raised her hand and straightened up. "I'm okay. Really. I just need to lay down."

"But you're not going to drive. If you start that rental car and gas is still floating around, you won't have to worry about selling the house because it'll be a big pile of blown-up rubble."

She had a point. "Okay, so will you please drive me to a motel?"

Finally, Donna relented and, though she really didn't need to, held her arm until Val got back to the car and sat down.

❖

It had begun to rain when Donna dropped her off at the Golden Shell Motel. It was a drive-in kind of establishment, where you passed under the carport next to the lobby and drove right up to your motel room. It had the usual sea decor, with fishing floats and netting nailed to the outside walls and draped over posts. It wasn't new, but it looked okay for one night. Three cars were pulled into spots, which left about nine or ten rooms vacant.

Donna pulled under the carport.

"Friends have stayed here before. It's not fancy, but it's cheap and clean," Donna said.

"Thanks again. For everything."

"You sure you don't want to come back to my place?"

"I'll be fine here."

"Call me if anything weird happens, okay?"

Val waved as Donna backed out and onto the highway and then made her way into the lobby. No one was behind the desk so she rang the bell on the counter. Its *ding* cut through the silence as if it was squawking at being woken up. After a minute or so, a tall thin man, dressed neatly in trousers and a button-down shirt, walked out from around a corner. He wore a pencil-thin mustache and his hair was a little mussed.

"Good evening."

He scrutinized her. "More like morning."

She glanced at the clock on the wall behind him. It was four a.m.

"I'd like a room, please."

"How many nights?"

"Just one."

"Where's your car?"

"Don't have one. I got dropped off."

He was in the middle of scrutinizing her choice of clothing when the phone rang.

"Golden Shell Motel," he said, then wrote something down on a piece of paper next to a logbook.

"Yes," he said, and picked up a clean white rag. He nearly attacked a smudge on the counter, attempting to polish it into oblivion. He looked at Val and then went back to his work. "Yes." He dug at the counter with the compulsion of a lunatic ridding his psychotic world of imaginary bugs.

This was one peculiar situation. She'd seen enough movies to know it wasn't smart to be a single woman checking into a motel in the middle of the night. In the rain, no less. The bizarre clerk made it all that more cinematically spooky.

He suddenly hung up and directed his rag to the phone.

"The room will be eighty-five dollars". He practically wiped the plastic off the receiver.

Val put her key ring down, reached into her wallet, and handed him a credit card. He seemed unwilling to conclude his phone cleansing, but with a seemingly forceful jerk of his hand, he cradled the receiver and began processing the charge on his computer.

Val looked around the lobby to avoid staring at him.

"This is a very clean motel," she said, hoping the small talk would help ease the tension she, at the very least, was feeling.

"Yes, it is."

"I can tell you take pride in that."

"It's very difficult in the inn business."

"Pardon?"

"To keep a motel clean. You'd be amazed at how dirty people are. The rooms are always a mess."

The clerk looked up from the computer and leaned toward Val. "People throw their trash everywhere but the trash can."

Val decided the safest response was to simply nod.

"Do you know what I find in the sheets?"

Val politely bent back from the waist, away from him. "I can imagine."

The clerk ignored her body language and tilted even farther toward her. The lines of his mouth tightened like an overly stretched rubber band.

"Sperm." He paused a beat as if the word were almost too difficult to pronounce. "And more."

Val suddenly found the whole situation rather funny and attempted to hide a guffaw. The only way to recover was to feign disgust.

"Hahaaaahhh…that's horrible."

"This is a motel, not a dirty brothel."

Val stared, wondering if any words could get him to finish her check-in any faster.

It was raining even harder now, and a rumble of thunder growled like a monster lurking outside in the dark.

If the gas leak didn't kill her, this motel might.

❖

Val opened the door to room number four, carrying with her the large manila envelope. She put it and her keys down on the dresser and surveyed the room. It was clean all right. It smelled strongly of pine though, which prodded her headache a bit.

She was glad the clerk had handed her the keys before he began attacking the computer with the rag. Otherwise, she might have been standing in the lobby the rest of the night.

Sitting down on the bed, she reflected over the past evening. It could have been worse, she thought, especially if she hadn't woken up. But where the hell was the gas leak? She had to wait until the next morning to see what the gas department said.

For now, though, she was tired and her head hurt. She needed to lie down for a while.

She turned her hands palms up and sighed.

"I have no toothbrush, no toothpaste, and no clean clothes."

Chapter Seven

Val slept until eight and then showered. She didn't like putting the same clothes back on, but she'd soon be at the house again and hopefully everything would return to normal.

She sat at the small desk in the corner of the room and opened the envelope. She pulled the paperwork out. Her mother's living trust was stapled into four different sections so she started with the first one.

"Agreement made April 11, 2008," Val read aloud. "This revocable living trust shall be known as the Kristine M. Montague Revocable Living Trust. Kristine M. Montague, called the grantor, declares that she has transferred and delivered to the trustee all her interest in the property described in Schedule A attached to this Declaration of Trust. All of that property is called the 'trust property.'…blahblahblah."

She rubbed her forehead.

"Upon the death or incapacity of Kristine M. Montague, the trustee of this trust and of any subtrusts created by it shall be Valerie S. Montague."

She skipped past the Bond, Compensation, and Liability sections.

"The trustee shall have all authority and powers allowed or conferred on a trustee under Oregon law, subject to the trustee's fiduciary duty to the grantors and the beneficiaries… yaddayaddayadda…The trustee's powers include, but are not limited to: The power to sell trust property, and to borrow money and to encumber trust property, including trust real estate, by mortgage, deed of trust or other method…The power to sell or grant options for the sale or exchange of any trust property, including stocks, bonds, debentures, and any other form of security or security account, at public or private sale for cash or on credit…"

This lawyerese was making her headache even worse. She stopped to rub her eyes and heard a quiet knock at the door.

She prayed it wasn't the clerk asking to clean her room. That would make it two places she couldn't go into.

She started to put down the section she was reading but dropped it. It fluttered to the floor so she quickly picked it up and stacked it neatly on top of the other sections before going to open the door.

Cam stood there, looking concerned.

"Cam!"

"Are you okay? I heard you were in the hospital."

"Yes, I'm fine now. Come in." She backed up and closed the door when Cam stepped through. "How'd you know I went to the hospital?"

"The night nurse has a thing for my morning hot chocolate."

"Okay, but how did you find me here?"

"Hemlock's not that big, Val." She gestured toward the lobby. "Plus, I used to work with the clean freak when we were short-order cooks. Many years ago. Anyway, I hope you don't mind."

Val laughed. "It's definitely okay."

"Are you sure you're feeling all right?"

She seemed genuinely concerned, which comforted Val. She'd been feeling pretty low, not to mention still a bit polluted from her natural-gas party.

"Yeah, I'm good, really. I was just killing time while I wait for the gas company."

"Then how about a fresh-cooked breakfast?"

❖

Cam took her back to the candy store and they went upstairs to her apartment. It was small and conveniently designed, with the front room opening up to a kitchen. A table made from salvaged timber separated the two rooms. Val sat at the table while Cam fried some eggs and bacon at the stove.

"I hope you don't mind eating here. I don't hire help during off-season since business is slow enough for me to handle. That means I'm here pretty much all day. A bell rings up here so I know when someone comes in."

"No, I don't mind at all." The bacon was beginning to rouse her hunger. The last thing she'd eaten was popcorn.

She looked around the tidy, eclectic apartment. The couch in the front room was framed in dark wood and upholstered in leather. It easily could have been made from twenty or thirty perfectly aged bomber jackets. The club chair nearby had a low back and was covered with plush, dark-green fabric. The heavy sides formed armrests that were a little lower than the back. A coffee table made from a large slab of wood that showed all its growth lines and cracks sat upon a metal nickel cross base. A braided jute, knobby-knitted rug and a flat-screen TV mounted to the wall completed the comfortable mood.

The kitchen was fairly modern, with brushed-nickel appliances housed between dark shaker cabinets. The counter was made from either quartz or granite, and its greenish tinge stood out nicely.

"How long have you lived here?"

Cam turned the eggs over. "I bought the building about five years ago but had to gut the apartment and renovate it. That took almost a year because I did it on my own."

"That's remarkable."

"I took my time because I was also running the shop. But it was fun."

"Did you make your furniture, too?"

"No. I'm not that talented. I found the slab of elm by the side of the road and took it to a guy that made it into the coffee table."

She filled Val's coffee cup and went back into the kitchen to get two plates from the cabinet. "And I saw the couch in Portland at a thrift store. It was caked with dirt and Lord knows what else. That one took me two weeks to thoroughly clean, but it was worth it."

"I really like your place. It's got a lot of personality."

"Thanks. I don't get much company but I'm glad you like it."

"You're not seeing anyone?"

"This isn't a great place to meet new people."

"I don't suppose the influx of tourists is a great place to look either."

"Not really, unless I was looking for a summer fling. Which I'm not."

"Do you talk with your ex? The one that's with Mack?"

"Not at all."

"Isn't it hard avoiding her?"

"Believe me, that's a whole lot easier than spending the last three years avoiding each other in the same bedroom."

Cam filled the plates with eggs and bacon and retrieved some utensils from a drawer. "What about you?"

"Enduringly single."

She put a plate and utensils down in front of Val and sat across from her. "That sounds like a self-help book."

Val laughed. "Maybe I should write it."

"Are you an expert?"

Val took a bite of the eggs. "I'm not really trying to be. My job has me traveling a lot."

"What do you do?"

"These eggs are really good." She picked up a piece of bacon and, before taking a bite, said, "I own a few designer antique stores."

"What's that exactly?"

"We sell antiques and repurposed items." Cam made the same blank face that a lot of people did, so she elaborated. "We take worn-out antiques, sometimes unusual items, and turn them into something that has another purpose. For instance, we've gutted used armoires and turned them into liquor cabinets and taken old feedbags and resewn them into throw pillows. We can repurpose a library card-catalog cabinet into a wine rack or a group of used clarinets and trumpets into garden fountains.

"I work with interior decorators that have clients all over the United States. We also have a large customer base so I'm fortunate to be able to travel a lot in search of great finds."

"Where do you live?"

"Dallas."

"Is that where you've been since high school?"

"Yeah. I went to the University of North Texas near Dallas. After I left here, I was pretty much on my own. My mom supported her boyfriend so she didn't have much left over. I worked full time and went to college when I could."

"How is it out there?"

"I like Texas. It can be a bit conservative, but Dallas is a fairly tolerant city."

"I've never been. Actually, I haven't even been out of Oregon, except for a few trips to Seattle." Cam took a sip of coffee. "I went to work straight out of high school. I've had just about every job you can have in a beach town. I waited tables, cleaned hotel rooms, stocked souvenir stores. I even roasted coffee beans in the middle of the night."

"You did?"

"I had the graveyard shift. I liked it because I didn't have to deal with people."

"The locals didn't give you a break even when you became an adult?"

"No. They talked about me a lot. They didn't trust me. That's part of the reason I had so many jobs. Plus, I liked the night shift because I could watch my little brother during the day. My parents weren't the best caregivers, and I'd make sure he had food. But anyway, I worked really hard, but all it took was somebody making a comment to my bosses and I had to bounce." She continued eating for a moment. "Anyway, the coffee place was my longest job. Mostly, I just worked my butt off, but I'd also stick around after the coffee shop opened for the day. I'd work for free into the morning so I could learn about running a business."

"That was clever."

Cam shrugged. "The only way I could ever control my surroundings was if I owned my own business."

"What about leaving Hemlock?"

"That wasn't possible."

"It wasn't?"

Cam looked down at her plate and then looked back up with a frail smile. "No."

The way her one-word answer came out reminded Val of air slowly escaping from a bald tire. She had no idea why Cam had never left town, but the thought tugged heavily in her chest.

"Would you like some more?" Cam said, pointing to her plate.

"No, thank you, I'm full." She put her fork down. "If I had more room for another pound or two of bacon, I'd take you up on it, though."

"Applewood bacon. It's the eighth deadly sin."

Val stood with her plate. "I don't want to keep you. And I need to get back to the house."

"Of course. Here, let me get that," Cam said and stood quickly, taking Val's plate with hers to the kitchen.

"Thank you so much for feeding me."

"I was happy to find you." Cam placed the dishes in the sink and reached for her keys.

"There's no need to drive me back, Cam. Your store's open and I can walk. It's not far."

"You're not walking. I can lock up, drive you to the motel, and be back in five minutes."

It wasn't that Val couldn't argue the logic; she just didn't want to. Cam was a refreshing, unexpected surprise.

"Would it be okay if you dropped me off at the house? It's almost ten, and I can get my rental car and drive over to the motel to check out later."

"Deal."

❖

Back at her mom's, Val walked up to the front door and opened it about an inch. She sniffed the air, hesitated, then stuck her head in, sniffing again. If a neighbor was watching they'd think she was immersed in some weird hallucination that she was a bloodhound on the hunt for a missing person.

She didn't smell anything and almost went inside, but just the memory of the dizziness and nausea made her sit down on the front steps.

The gas-company truck pulled up about ten thirty, and she waited while the service technician went through the house. After about ten minutes, he exited and approached her.

"I found the problem and turned the gas back on." He paused as he wrote a note on the clipboard he held. "You left your burner on."

"The burner? On the stove?"

"Yes, ma'am." He continued writing.

"I haven't cooked anything at all."

"Maybe your husband or kid did." He tore off a copy of whatever he was writing on. "I shut the knob off and found no other leak. The house is fine to reenter."

"But I didn't use the stove."

The technician's interest in her story was akin to a politician's concern for the little guy. He handed the form to her and told her to have a good day.

❖

Val went back to the front door, and this time she threw it open. Closing it behind her, she looked around the rooms. She wasn't really searching for anything; she just needed a minute to collect her thoughts.

The stove burner had been on. How could that be? Had she accidentally bumped into the knob the last time she was in there? Even if the burner hadn't ignited, she would have heard the *tick, tick, tick* of the starter. Wouldn't she?

Val walked into the kitchen and turned one of the knobs. It ticked until a flame caught and rolled around the circle of metal. She turned the burner off and tried the other three. They all performed the same way.

Testing her theory, she twisted a knob, but just barely, as if she'd just bumped it. It ticked at the slightest turn.

Unsatisfied, she turned it back off and stared at the stove. Finally, she said "To hell with it" and went into the garage to get in her rental car.

She'd be happy never to touch that stove again.

❖

As Val was parking at the motel, she noticed something hanging from her door. She got out and walked up to a little brown bag, tied around the doorknob by a string. She untied it and peeked inside.

The colorful assortment of taffy could have been a real rainbow in a bag. She grinned, thinking that Cam was probably the nicest person she'd ever met. Plucking a piece out, she unwrapped it and unlocked the door.

With a short throw, her keys landed on the unmade bed. She checked her watch and looked at the motel card on the back of the door. Checkout time was eleven thirty. She had thirty minutes.

Val chewed on the taffy, which started out with a vanilla taste but ended with a burst of cinnamon that made her grin.

"Cozy as it is," she said, looking around the room, "I must leave you."

She had nothing to pack so she walked over to scoop up the manila envelope when she stopped cold. Someone had gone through the paperwork. She remembered stacking the sections neatly before opening the door for Cam, but now they were askew, the sections fanned out just slightly.

She snatched up the pile and sorted through it.

A frantic jolt of concern shot up her neck. "Who's been in here?"

She looked around the room. Maybe it was the maid. Val dashed into the bathroom, but her towel was still on the floor and the soap by the sink was wet. She came back out and stared at her keys lying on the unmade bed. Her body went rigid in confusion.

"Shit," she said.

Picking up her belongings, she dialed a number on her cell phone and left the room.

❖

"Thanks for meeting me, Donna."

Val sat across from her at the Halfway Cafe.

"I still don't understand." Donna sipped on her glass of water.

"Someone's going through my things. My drawer in my kitchen, my nightstand. It's really strange."

"But you had people visiting during Nedra's open house. I wouldn't call a few things out of place strange."

"And someone went through my things at the motel."

Donna paused, studying her. She reached over and put her hand over Val's. "You had a gas cocktail last night, Val. I wouldn't be surprised if you saw little green men, too."

"I'm serious, Donna."

"Okay, okay." She thought for a moment. "What about the maid in the motel room?"

"The maid hadn't even started cleaning yet."

"Look, I was the only one who knew you were at the motel. Just me."

"Cam knew."

"Cam? Nelson?"

"Yes. From high school."

Donna began to say something but just shook her head.

"What?"

"I don't know, Val. She's been trouble ever since we were young. There's a reason everyone used to call her the bad seed. Still do."

"This is so weird."

"Listen. I just think a couple of random things happened and you're connecting them. I wasn't joking about the gas. You were just in the hospital, for God sakes. You're dealing with your mother's death and selling her house. I think you're really stressed, Val."

Val stared into her coffee.

"Still," Donna added, "I'd stay away from Cam. No one in town trusts her."

Val's head still hurt. Donna was right. It had been less than twenty-four hours since she'd been in the hospital. How long had it been since she took some aspirin? She reached up to rub her head.

"You miss your mom, don't you?"

Val looked up at Donna. "Yes."

"Kris was a wonderful woman. I wish you could have gotten back here more often. She was involved in the little community theater. I saw a couple of articles in the local paper about her, too. Did she send them to you?"

Val started to cry. It finally hit her. Her mom was dead. She wanted to wail out her grief but tightened her chest, trying to hold in as much as she could.

"Val, honey, I'm sorry I brought it up…"

"It's okay," she blubbered. "Up to now, I guess I've been too busy to cry much." She wiped her eyes. "You're right. I should have come here more often. Mom and I hardly spoke…but I always thought we'd have…more time."

"Don't blame yourself."

"It's easy to get too busy with your life." She began to cry harder, the guilt slicing through her like an arctic wind on bare skin. "I never told her enough how much I loved her."

Donna rubbed Val's shoulder and then gently coaxed her out of the chair. She left some money on the table and led her outside.

Donna had her arm around Val and was guiding her.

Val pointed. "My car's over there."

"I know. But you're coming with me."

"Where are we going?"

"Just shut up."

❖

Donna pulled up in front of a church. Val caught the sign out front just as they were passing it. Carved out of wood, the sign was painted white and light blue. It read, THE SEEDS OF LIGHT CHURCH.

"What are we doing here?"

Donna parked near the entrance. The church lot was half full.

"Come on."

Donna got out of the car, and after a beat, she followed.

When they stepped inside, a man stood at the pulpit and a service was underway.

"We think of light as bright and obvious," the man up front was saying. "But the existence of candles, and even fireflies, demonstrates that just a little light can make a great difference. An intriguing image is found in Psalm 97:11." He raised his hand. "*Light is sown for the righteous, and gladness for the upright in heart.*"

He had altered his voice for the passage, making it almost quiver, and Val found it a little phony.

"Light is sown," he said, "like little seeds being scattered over a field. Can you see it? We are asked to live in a way that pleases God. We are those little seeds of light."

Val listened as she looked around the room. She was surprised at how plain it was. The pews were simple rows of wooden benches with simple backs. The windows were void of stained glass but were covered with light-brown drapes instead. There was a beautifully made wooden pulpit and a low table-like altar, but otherwise the area was relatively unadorned. And only one very simple cross hung on the back wall.

The pastor raised his voice. "When our brothers and sisters bring their young to the steps outside this holy place and encourage them to walk by themselves, to talk to the pastor by themselves, they are sowing the seeds of light. When the parents of a five-year-old entrust the Sunday-school teacher to keep him at the church, even late into the night sometimes, they are sowing seeds of light."

"That was weird," Val said under her breath.

Donna leaned toward her. "What?"

"Nothing. Hey, what are we doing here?"

The pastor's hands flew up and he almost yelled. "We are spiritual beings in flesh. Worship…is the touching of one spirit with another. We touch each other and see our seeds being sown. Go in peace to love and serve the church and one another."

"It's what *you're* going to do."

"What is that?"

"This was your mom's church."

Val looked away and watched the parishioners rising from the pews and start filing out. They passed them, and Val tried to picture her mom among them, sitting in one of the pews or walking down the aisle. She felt the dull ache of loss wash through her body and wished she could see her right then. The ache of missing her amplified the regret that she had never mended their relationship. As the tears came again, she wondered if she'd ever run out of them.

"She came here all the time," Donna said. "She was at services, and she even volunteered here." Donna gave Val a gentle push. "And you're going to sit down and talk to her."

Val took a seat, and Donna quietly walked off somewhere, leaving her alone. The last of the parishioners were leaving, and the echoes of footsteps leading out the door finally faded, leaving Val in silence.

The drapes of one window were drawn open. The sky was gray, and though she couldn't hear it from where she sat, the wind rustled the pine trees, making them look as if they were huddled together, gossiping.

She turned to face the altar and closed her eyes. She wasn't a church-going person and rarely called to a higher power. She lived as good a life as she could and figured she didn't need to sit in an organized meeting and share her private beliefs. She never really prayed, per se. She often talked to herself, playing the mother and the child, discussing her actions and righting her wrongs. It helped guide her and allowed her to see what was best. But it was more like meditation than praying.

Still, since she was sitting here, she tried.

"I miss you, Mom," she said to herself. "I really miss you. I wish I had come back more often." Tears freely flowed down her face now.

"Your house is so…empty. Part of me wants to move in just to be closer to you. I know it's too late, and I'm sorry. I don't think I had much of a choice when I graduated from high school."

She wiped her closed eyes. "I know you needed to have your own life and that Chuck was—"

A calm voice spoke beside her. “You must be Val.”

She opened her eyes. A man in a collared shirt stood over her. He also had on jeans and tennis shoes. His dark hair had a crisp and conservative crop, the kind meant to either control unruly growth or convey a style choice that wasn’t quite hip. He wore a leather necklace tied to a small silver tooth that hung below his white collar band and an ecology pin fastened to his shirt. He had to be in his late thirties or early forties. Funky would almost describe him.

“I’m Pastor Kind.”

“Hi.” Self-consciously, Val wiped her tears.

“You don’t have to do that. Crying is allowed here.”

Val sniffed and nodded.

“I have to confess, Donna sent me out here.”

“Hi.” She put her hand out, not sure if she should shake his hand or kiss a ring or something.

He grasped her hand and placed his other one on top of theirs. “Donna cares about you and said you’re feeling a little punk right now. I’m so sorry your mother was called up. But if I may tell you, Kris had a magnificent, full life. She was doing what she wanted. And so were you, don’t forget. I know you feel badly that you weren’t here when she died. That’s the way it was meant to be. And you can’t change that now. What you can do is still talk to her. She’ll hear you.”

“I just was…kind of.”

“Consider her your connection.” He released a hand and pointed toward the ceiling. “Up there!”

“Thanks.”

“Are you taking care of her affairs?”

“Yes. It’s just that it seems so…strange, coming down here to get rid of her things and close out her bank account.”

“I guarantee you, she doesn’t care. As a matter of fact, I’m sure she’s glad you’re staying at her house.”

Val took in his words.

“Have you decided what you’ll be doing with the house?”

“It’s for sale.”

“Again, she won’t mind.”

"I know, I guess."

The pastor looked up as if he were contemplating something. "Say, tell me the last thing she said to you."

"Ah, we talked on the phone maybe a few months ago." It felt awful to admit that much time had passed without contact.

"And what did you talk about?"

"We…I think we talked about my work. And a play she was just finishing."

"Anything else?"

"She…was concerned about something."

"What?"

Val paused, not really sure why he was asking these questions.

"I don't quite remember. It had something to do with some people she knew."

"Friends?"

"I suppose. She named them, but I can't remember now."

"Was it a bad thing? Was she worried?"

Awkwardness began to permeate the conversation. Did men of the cloth usually talk more than newscasters after a political scandal? "She was concerned," Val said slowly. "I'd say she was worried.

"What did she say was bothering her?"

"I'm not sure why you're asking me this."

The pastor smiled. "What I'm getting at are two things. First, whatever was bothering her, no longer is. She's in a place of rest and serenity. Second, I want you to remember as much as you can about your mother. Relive all your moments with her. Keep her alive in your heart. Heed the advice she gave you growing up and laugh again at the funny things she said."

He put a hand on her shoulder. "And even cry when you want."

❖

Val found Donna sitting in the pew with her eyes closed.

"I'm ready to go now."

Donna jumped slightly and then rose to walk with Val out of the church.

"How was it?"

"Talking with Mom or the pastor you sicced on me?"

"Didn't he make you feel better?"

She wasn't sure because she wasn't used to churches, or pastors, or even praying, for that matter. He was nice with a soft-spoken voice whose volume was probably always set on soft, except for his turn at the pulpit. "I suppose."

"He's a good ear, if you ever need one."

❖

Donna dropped Val off at her car.

"Thanks for caring, Donna," Val said as she closed the door and leaned against the frame of the open window.

"What are friends for? Hey, do you have plans later?"

"I think it'll be a quiet night at home for me. I'm still pretty tired from the whole day."

"Okay, have a great evening. Call if you need anything." Donna waved to Val as she drove away.

Val lifted her hand unenthusiastically. Her grief was probably catching up with her. Thinking about her mother—spending conscious thought and deliberate consideration about her mother's life, their strained relationship, and her untimely end—had taken a lot out of her.

She was really beginning to dislike the empty house. And she was equally unwilling to go to bed early because she knew she'd wake up at one or two in the morning. If she did, she would stare at the ceiling as if it were a blank screen on which she would picture more of her confusing and frustrating childhood and her life since, spent without much contact with her mother, until the sun broke free of the Oregon coastal fog and pushed her out of bed.

So she sat on the couch. The manila envelope containing her mother's living trust sat across from her on the coffee table. She stared at the stack of paper. A simple pile of wood pulp had been turned into paper sheets that now possessed serious meaning and function. It was an important document, a statement of finality, demanding to be put into practice.

The living trust, Val thought, a written document of insurance for those who wanted to have some semblance of control in their posthumous years, to bequeath or deny whatever they chose, to set forth a decree commanding the specific disbursement of what they had owned while in the flesh of life, so that their wishes were specifically carried out long past their ability to personally ensure their demands were met with satisfaction. Long past the stiffness of rigor mortis and the disposal of the flesh, the bequeather was still able to reach out a spectral hand and ensure that because of their lawyer-approved terms of property distribution, the material goods they wished to convey fell safely into the hands of their chosen recipients.

This living trust, intentionally meant to lie as dormant as a fourteen-year cicada lies still beneath the earth, waited for the moment it was freed to become useful and serve a purpose. And the time of death, according to the living trust, became that certain cicada spring, and the lawyer became the vessel that called it forth when, finally, their now-departed, out-of-print edition of themselves could rest easy, assured their last biddings had been granted.

All that hoopla, Val thought, for a mother to pass along her possessions to her only child.

Had she been able to talk to her mother about her end-of-life plans, she would have told her that she didn't want the house and didn't need whatever savings were left in her bank account. Val would have told her that she'd moved on long ago, that her mother's possessions should remain with whatever boyfriend was hers that particular year or, barring a beau, that any afterlife assets should go to whatever charity her mother found most appropriate.

But her mother had thought differently. And she had immortalized in ink that she had apparently always wanted Val to have it all.

Maybe the reason was wrapped up in her mother's desire to get Val to return to Hemlock for whatever motive she'd carried with her. Or possibly she'd left Val her possessions out of guilt for running her off right after graduation.

But then again, perhaps forcing her to return to Hemlock was designed to be the penance for leaving in the first place.

Part of Val reasoned that leaving her things to her daughter made perfect sense, but then why do so when Val had clearly not been present during the majority of the last two decades of her life?

The living trust sat on a glass-topped coffee table, and she figured she'd eventually need to read it all. Underneath the glass lay two tattered-edge photo albums. Val reached down, hefted their bulky weight, and dropped them on her lap.

According to the wording, neatly written in pen on the inside cover, the contents contained a chronological record of the past five years of her mother's life in Hemlock. Most of the pages stored newspaper clippings of her involvement in the local community theater. Photos and articles with pink highlights underlined her name or character.

Val stopped at one that read "*The Girls From The Garden Club* guaranteed to harvest the laughs!" Another had a picture of her mother and two other cast members with a byline declaring "*The Girls From The Garden Club* soak up rays of sunshine!" Another article gave the play a rave review: "For a relatively small play, *The Girls From The Garden Club* hits big!" Reading further down, Val found the pink highlight mentioning her mother. "Kris Montague's run as Rhoda is endearing and funny. It is also to be noted that she served as the play's prop person. 'It's fun to try to get as many props as you can on a shoestring budget,' she said."

The sting of the first tears of sadness nipped at the inside corners of her eyes. She allowed them easy passage, and they ran down the sides of her nose, streaming down her face, where they pooled on the tip of her chin until she wiped them away.

She looked up at the ceiling. "Oh, Mom. You were living your life, weren't you? You were having a blast and just doing your thing."

Val sifted through more pictures and articles. She smiled and even chuckled at times, then raised her hand to her chest as if trying to quell the physical throb of guilt because she hadn't experienced that part of her life with her mother.

A cracking sound came from outside and Val jumped. She listened for something else that would give her more information as to the origin of the sound, but only silence followed. Still, the noise had been pronounced enough that she decided to get up to investigate. She flicked her wrist over. It was after nine o'clock, which wasn't late, but the racket had been so out of the ordinary, given that the whole time she'd been home prior, the din from the sporadic traffic on the highway was the only audible activity.

She stopped at the front door, listening again. She reached for the doorknob and heard scuffling. It sounded close.

Val spoke through the closed door. "Hello?"

When her call went unanswered, she went to the front window and looked out. Seeing nothing out of the ordinary, she opened the front door and peered outside. The street was dark, as usual, her car sitting exactly as she'd parked it in the driveway and the lamppost right by her door illuminating the first third of the front lawn.

She turned to go back inside, and in that same second, she heard a swooshing sound. Her brain reacted by turning to her right, but a shroud of white instantly seized her entire upper body.

She raised her arms, not understanding what was happening, but aggressive hands apprehended them, yanking them downward as the pungent smell of laundry soap attacked her nostrils. As the cloth constricted her face and throat, she realized it must have been a pillowcase and it was now excessively tight.

The terrified panic of a scuba diver reaching for an air tank filled her, and somehow, she flailed enough to get one hand free and grabbed the cloth. She was able to lift part of the pillowcase off her head so she could see two sets of shoes. A pair of Dingo boots was right in front of her, matching her frightened twisting, and suddenly, the reality of her situation slammed home.

Thrashing as violently as she could, she fought to break away. She then screamed, but the attempt morphed into a grunt when she was thrown backward, to the ground just inside her foyer. All she could see were legs and belt buckles before the pillowcase was shoved down to her throat again.

A growl came from one of the men, and she could almost feel his breath through the cloth. "Shut up!"

The words felt like a poisonous snake threatening to strike her at close range, and her automatic reflex was to twist and push away powerfully. Self-preservation became her only drive, and she contorted her body frantically.

A series of punches that came fast and hard rewarded her. The first ones glanced off her shoulder and arm, but then they began to land with ferocious accuracy. Her chest took two blows that knocked the breath out of her, and two sets of fists simultaneously pummeled her shoulders and head, immobilizing her. She crumpled to the ground, and they landed on top of her.

She heard a voice, though she wasn't sure if it was the same man as before. "Go."

One of them raised himself off her. Footsteps clomped loudly and quickly around the house. With one of the men holding her down roughly, and her entire upper body aching from the blows, all she could do was listen.

Other sounds came, and she knew he was rummaging round the house. A rush of anguish washed over her as telltale signs of drawers opening and things being moved around came from all the rooms.

And then she heard jingling.

Val tried to scream, but the man's weight forced her breath into a grunt. She managed to get out a few words. "What do you want?"

The man hit her again.

"I said shut up, bitch! Just shut up!"

More shuffling and movement came, and the stomping of boots got louder. She rolled her head just as a fist came down on the side of her face. White fireworks exploded behind her closed eyes. She tried to roll into a ball and realized she could because the hands that had held her had let go.

She heard the men leave through the front door. Val reached up to remove the pillowcase and yelped at the pain in her ribcage. She dropped the pillowcase at her side and quickly scanned the house to make sure they were really gone. She tried to lift herself off the floor, but the pain seared her all over and her legs shook too much.

The door was wide open and she crawled toward it. She didn't see anything on the darkened street in front of her house, but then headlights flashed on and a car pulled up by the for-sale sign.

Rage bubbled up from her stomach, and she struggled to yell out her anger but couldn't. The two men jumped into the car, and though the interior lights came on, she couldn't make out much detail about them. But in the three seconds it took them to slam the doors and extinguish the light, she made out one startling detail. The person sitting in the front passenger seat was the woman whose Buick had hit the deer first.

As the car sped away, Val rolled onto her back and stared at the ceiling. She moved her hand toward her front pocket and winced. Slowly, she pulled her phone out, dialed 911, and told the woman who answered what had happened. Val was told to stay on the line. What else could she do? She lay there on the floor and continued to stare at the ceiling, wondering what the fuck those guys had stolen from the house.

❖

The police officer had just taken her report while his partner roamed around the front yard looking for evidence. The other one stood close by, writing in a small notebook. Donna sat with Val on the couch as two paramedics finished treating a cut over her eyebrow.

"I don't understand this," she said aloud, though she wasn't really addressing anyone in particular.

"I don't either," Donna said, "but I know you shouldn't be staying here anymore."

"What I shouldn't be doing is answering the door."

One of the paramedics stood from her kneeling position in front of Val. "You really should go to the hospital."

"No, I don't want to."

"Okay," she said. "We're all finished here. But if your ribs get worse or you wake up and have trouble breathing tomorrow, you'll need to go see a doctor."

Val reached up and tentatively touched her bandaged forehead. "Thank you."

"We don't get many home invasions around here," the policeman said as he finished writing. "If you're able to, could you look around and see what they took?"

With help from Donna, Val got up slowly and walked through the house. Breathing hurt like hell. The paramedics said they didn't think anything was broken, but her body felt like it had run with the Pamplona bulls and unceremoniously lost.

The place did look tossed around. Drawers and cabinets were left open and items in the closets were overturned. But her mother's valuables, which were mostly inexpensive rings and necklaces, were still in her dresser drawer.

"Nothing's missing that I can tell," she said when she returned to the front room.

The officer who'd been outside stepped back in through the front door and shook his head. The first officer closed his notebook and handed Val a business card. "We'll be stopping by Mack's garage tomorrow morning, Miss Montague. Since he's working on the car of the woman you saw, he should have her name and number."

"Mack knows her, too," Val said as she sat back down next to Donna.

"All the better."

The paramedics began wrapping up their work. A knock at the open door made them all turn their heads. Pastor Kind walked in and greeted both officers by their first names. He nodded to the paramedics, thanking one for helping some elderly church member with his bad knee, then walked over to Val.

"Are you all right?"

"This town is getting smaller by the minute."

Donna swatted Val on the knee. "I called him, you dork."

"I'm here to help," Pastor Kind said. "Unfortunately, I know more than I care to about trouble. I serve on the Hemlock Violence Abatement Council here. Some of us townsfolk spend time reading the violence reports at the police station and carry the word, as well as the awareness, out to the streets."

The officers walked to the doorway. “We’re through here. Miss Montague, my number is on that business card as well as the case number that you can refer to. I doubt they’ll be back tonight, but if you see these people again, don’t go outside. Call 911.”

“Lesson learned. Thank you.”

Pastor Kind waved to the officers as they walked out and then sat down on Val’s other side.

She felt confined, and a thought ran through her mind of a mosquito between two hands slapped quickly together.

“Tell me what you saw,” Pastor Kind said.

“Just like I told the officer, I heard some noise outside the front door, and when I opened it, two men grabbed me. They threw a pillowcase over my head, and one of them started beating the crap out of me.”

“What did the other one do?”

“I’m not sure, but it sounded like he was looking for something. All I could hear…” She stopped suddenly. “The jingling!”

Val got up a little too quickly. She felt Donna’s hand on her arm as she closed her eyes and waited for the dizziness to stop.

“This is the second time you’ve almost passed out,” Donna said.

She tried to pull her back down to the couch, but Val waved her off and sluggishly walked over to the dining-room table.

“The keys. Goddamn it.”

“What?”

“The keys. They took my mother’s keys.”

Donna stood. “What would they want with them?”

“I have no clue.

Pastor Kind asked, “Did you have anything special on the key ring?”

“Not unless they coveted my mom’s little Kewpie doll.”

Donna looked sideways at Val. “No, he means what did the keys go to?”

“Just this house. My mom’s safe-deposit-box key.” She shook her head, baffled. “The car key wasn’t on there. It’s at Mack’s.” She sat down at the table. “Maybe they wanted to steal the rental car and broke in to steal the keys because they never learned how to hot-wire."

Pastor Kind's voice was hesitant. "You're joking again, huh?"

"Yes."

"Did they get that key?"

"No. It's still in my pocket. They were too stupid to check, I guess."

"What about your mother's safe-deposit box?" Donna asked. "Maybe these guys wanted jewelry or other valuables."

"Do you know what's in it?" Pastor Kind said.

"Nothing now. This just doesn't make sense." She looked up at the pastor. "Any similar crime patterns come to mind?"

"No. This one's new. If this is a home-invasion crime, it's a pretty subdued one. And nothing else was on the key ring?"

"No."

"Well, I hope this is the first and last time someone invades your place."

"This wasn't the first time."

"What do you mean?"

Donna answered for her. "Someone went through some of Val's things during the open house Nedra Tobias had the other day. And at the motel, too."

Her stare at Val was stern, and she suddenly realized the intent.

Donna continued. "Cam Nelson knew you were at the motel. You told me so at lunch today."

Would Cam do that, Val wondered.

Pastor Kind said, "What do you think Cam would want?"

"I don't know."

"Maybe she knows about your mother's living trust. Money makes people do strange things."

Val flicked her wrist like a gambler waves off another card. "It's a living trust. She can't touch it."

"Still," Donna said, "you'd better stay away from her for a while. At least until the police can sort things out."

The pastor got up and walked over to Val. "I'll call the police and tell them they might want to pay Cam a visit."

He placed a reassuring hand on Val's shoulder, but all she felt was uncomfortable.

"The police will find out who did this," he said.

"Do you want me to stay tonight?"

"No, Donna. I'm fine. You two go home. I just need some sleep."

"Well, I guess you've had enough excitement for one night." Donna stood.

Val nodded. "Whoever said that Hemlock was a boring little town?"

"You did, twenty years ago. The day you left."

Donna hugged her and then followed Pastor Kind to the front door.

"Call me if anything weird happens, okay?"

"That's the second time you've had to say that," Val said and closed the door behind them.

❖

Val lay on the couch, a hand draped over her bandaged forehead. Why were these things happening? What did they want? Were they just slimy riffraff who knew her mom was dead and figured they could just scare off the foreigner daughter and take what they wanted?

She sat up slowly and assessed the ache in her head. She could handle the dull throbbing and even the nasty pain in her ribs, but what would it feel like come morning?

The photo album she'd been looking through right before she was beaten up was still open. She picked it up and put it in her lap. She flipped through the pages but couldn't concentrate on any one image. When she reached the last page, she put the album aside and picked up the other one.

The pages held childhood memories documenting the time she'd lived in Hemlock.

"Something's going on, Mom. What do they want?"

She looked at a photo of her mom helping her get a bowl from a cupboard in the kitchen. Val was probably six and her mom was holding her up. In it, Val clutched the bowl, her face full of victory.

"I wish I could have helped you." Val touched the picture. "I should have been there when your heart started hurting. Maybe I could have gotten you to the hospital faster. I should have done something."

She looked up from the image and said, "Maybe I can now."

On the counter of a sideboard in the living room sat a pile of recent mail, a few stacked books, and a flower growing in a pot. For a moment she paused and stared at the sideboard mirror. She reached up and touched the bandage, then pushed her fingers into her eyebrows to relieve some of the ache.

The phone book lay in the top drawer, and she fished it out and dropped it on top of the sideboard. Staring at it as if it was supposed to tell her something, she waited.

"Should I?" she said.

The phone book didn't respond.

"What the fuck should I do?"

With a fist she gently punched the cover, prodding it for more of an answer than just people's names and numbers.

Pushing off from the sideboard, she turned and held her side, gingerly pacing the living room.

One call could help. But then again, it could be a huge mistake.

Returning to the phone book, she finally opened it and searched for a listing. Her heart beat faster as she dialed.

"Hi," she said, her throat feeling suddenly so dry she might cough. "I know this might sound strange, but I need your help."

CHAPTER EIGHT

When the doorbell rang, Val jumped as if not expecting it. But in truth, she was nervous *because* she was expecting it. She opened the door.

The perfectly cute smile suddenly dropped from Cam's face. She stepped in. "What happened to you?"

Val led her inside and walked toward the couch. "I was attacked tonight."

"What?"

Val wasn't one of those face readers, but Cam seemed to be genuinely surprised.

"The police called it a type of home-invasion robbery."

"My God, are you all right?" Cam sat when Val did.

"Yes, but I'm more confused than injured."

"What do you mean?"

"Something very bizarre is going on, Cam. Sunday, during the open house here, someone rummaged through my things. Then Tuesday, while I was at your house for breakfast, someone got into that motel room and did the same." She pointed to her forehead. "Now this. These guys came in and stole my keys."

Cam's eyebrows crunched together like two thin caterpillars arching up in ire. "Fuck," she said quickly. The caterpillars stayed where they were. "I don't understand what's going on."

"They were looking for something."

"Like, to steal your car?"

"I don't know. Whatever it is, they're determined to get it."

"Did they take anything else? Money?"

"No."

Cam's jaw tightened. "Those assholes beat you up for your car keys?"

Val nodded. "And one of the people in the car that they drove was that girl I got into the car accident with."

"Are you serious?"

"Strange, huh?"

"Do you know her name?"

"Not her last name. All I remember is Cindy."

Cam shook her head. "That doesn't ring any bells. But I'm not surprised. People roll through here all the time, hitchhiking up and down the coast and stuff."

Val closed one eye and rubbed her head, and Cam said, "How much does it hurt?"

"Like a twelve-pack hangover."

Cam got up, looked around the room, and headed for the kitchen. "I'm going to get you some aspirin."

"That's okay, really."

She could hear Cam opening a cabinet and running the faucet.

"Here. Take this," she said as she came out, holding a glass. "Bathroom?"

Val began to get up and she waved her off, so Val pointed.

A moment later Cam came back and held her hand out, palm down.

Val reached up and caught two aspirin.

"That's it," Cam said. "Give me your phone."

She took it and typed, saying, "Here's my cell number. I should have given it to you earlier."

"Thanks." Val popped the pills into her mouth and drank some water.

"You know," Cam said, "I've been thinking about what you told me at breakfast. That the gas company said the leak was from the stove burner being on. If it'd been on since your mother's death, you would have smelled it the moment you first came into the house."

Val swallowed some more water and put the glass down. "I know. And I didn't. I haven't touched the stove since I've been here."

"Do you think someone did it deliberately to get you out of here?"

Val shook her head. "I don't know."

Cam sat down and squeezed her hand. Val still wasn't sure if she should believe what Donna had said. Maybe she couldn't trust Cam. She'd certainly steered clear of her in high school. But most of her class would have done the same to her if they'd known she was gay.

Cam's hand felt warm and strong. Should she trust her?

"I need your help." She told herself she needed to closely watch Cam, just in case.

"Name it."

"I don't think that seeing the girl Cindy tonight was a coincidence."

"Okay. So what's the connection?" Cam's hand remained curled around Val's.

She'd heard somewhere that if two people held hands, it would be that much more difficult to yell at each other. Did that philosophy apply to lying, as well?

"So you and the girl have an accident," Cam said, "and she then gets your address from Mack's, and she and her buddies set out to rob you of…something."

"I know, it's plausible, but it's full of holes."

"The biggest being why?"

"I just can't figure out what they wanted. Or still want. Whatever it is, they've tried three times and haven't gotten it."

"I'd put my money on the possibility that Mack's involved."

"Why do you think that?"

"Well, you might think it's because I'm pissed that my ex cheated on me with Mack," Cam said. "Okay, that's pretty much it. But I didn't like Mack before. He's an ass and a bully. He's pretty much a pig of a man, plus he's a bit weird."

"Any more than pretty much everyone else in this town?"

Cam smiled.

"Maybe they've got some sort of theft ring going on." Val doubted it as soon as she said it. "What do I know? This town is probably too small to do something like that unnoticed."

"I wouldn't rule anything out at this point. Did you tell the police?"

"No. Not yet."

"I think you should call them. Now. I mean, really, Val. This is bad."

Val doubted Cam would have said that if she were also somehow involved. But Donna was pretty adamant about Cam's shady past.

"That's not the worst part," Val said.

Cam put her other hand over Val's. The gentle squeeze felt reassuring.

"What else did they do?"

"It's not what they did. It's what my friend did."

Cam waited, her eyes fixed on her.

Val reached for the manila envelope and held it up. "She told me that all of this might be because of my mother's living trust. She left me some money."

"That's feasible."

"I never told her about mom's living trust. It's been sitting in a safe-deposit box for almost five years."

Cam's expression shifted slightly, as if it were an expanding balloon filling with a little more air.

"But," Cam said, "maybe your mom told her about it."

"They weren't really friends. They probably saw each other out at the store or something, but Mom wouldn't have associated with her."

"Do you think she's involved in this?"

Val stared at the coffee table, almost afraid to admit it and wondering if the blow to the head or the gas episode might have jumbled her noggin. "I hope she's not. We grew up together. We went to grade school, junior high, and high school together. I haven't really been close to her in twenty years, but I just can't believe she could be tangled up in this." She looked up at Cam, whose face seemed to be filled with authentic concern. "But if she is," Val added, "I need to know.

"I think it's time we let the police handle it."

Val wasn't sure if Cam's reference to "we" was sincere, but she hoped so.

"I've got to find out for myself," she told Cam. "If all the police do is arrest that girl and those guys that beat me up, I might never know what they wanted or if Donna was involved."

Cam suddenly looked shaken. She hesitated, as if a ghost had just flown past them.

"What's wrong?"

"Donna," Cam said, as if she hadn't heard right.

"Yes…"

"Donna Laufstrom?"

She nodded. "From high school. Why?"

"Val," Cam said slowly, "Donna's my ex."

Val stared at Cam. "Donna…?"

"Donna's seeing Mack. He's the one Donna cheated on me with."

"You're serious."

Cam's silence answered loudly.

"You were with Donna?"

"Yeah. And I guess you were too. You two were more than just close in high school."

Val looked at Cam, who dipped her head and stared through her eyebrows, challenging her.

"It was obvious to me." Cam looked down at her hands and squeezed Val's. "The plot thickens, doesn't it?"

"I wish this were just a book. That way, I'd be sitting somewhere, like on a plane or at the beach, reading about some bizarre situation and being glad it wasn't my life."

"Welcome to the 45th parallel."

Val smiled. "It was the coffee mug, wasn't it?"

"Yup. Shouldn't have bought it. Now you're cursed." Cam's smile, which was a little crooked, reminded Val of a lopsided bow tie on a little kid. "What do you want to do, Val?"

What did she want to do? How about go back to the airport and forget this all happened? Or how about wishing her mother hadn't died and that she'd visited her more often so she'd know what the hell was going on in this town? The photo albums still lay on the coffee table, and she focused on the one that was open. The photographs were taken when Val was about ten. One in particular was of Val and her mother in the kitchen, her mother holding up a bag of chocolate-chip cookies. Val remembered the picture because right before it was taken, her mother had told her to act like they were famous chefs. She and her mom had stood tall and stared seriously into the camera. Val smiled at the memory.

If she could only go back.

"I know what I want to do." She looked up at Cam. "Go back to the beginning."

"The beginning," Cam said, looking at her as if trying to read her mind. Slowly, she began to nod. "You want to go to Mack's garage. To the car."

"Yes. It all seems to have started there. Something's going on. I can't explain it and I have absolutely no proof, but if I don't take a step forward, I'll just be waiting for someone else to run me over."

Val searched Cam's eyes for a hint of hesitancy or some kind of dubious caution, but she saw the bright-eyed gaze of concurrence. Val nodded as if giving the command to drop the bomb.

Cam laughed and leaned forward until their faces were inches away, and Val's breath caught in her throat. Cam reached up, and her soft fingers stroked the area around her bandaged forehead. Slowly, gently, she moved closer and placed a sweet, innocent, but drawn-out kiss on her lips.

And it was perfect. Val felt the warmth of Cam's lips and the sincerity of her intentions. It was not too much but enough to say, "I like you."

Val placed her hand on Cam's cheek. Her soft skin was as warm as her lips, and the deep desire to explore her whole face and neck, to take in all the details of her beautiful face, pulled at her with a force she hadn't felt in years. Since her last breakup, many desires had deserted her and, until now, had failed to return. But

Cam brought them back as a slow spark, promising to ignite a dry pile of kindling.

She let her fingers linger on Cam's cheek before pulling slowly away. "I haven't been kissed like that in a long time."

Cam opened her mouth to say something and Val held her breath, waiting because it seemed that the look in her eyes boiled with as much desire as she suddenly felt between her legs.

As unexpectedly as a drop of unforeseen rain splashes on someone's nose, Cam's expression appeared to jump in reaction. "Those bastards. Let's go."

The letdown jarred Val. Maybe she'd gotten too far ahead of herself. Cam might not have the same feelings at all. Val had experienced both directions of a one-way street many times, and now she just might be facing the wrong way.

She forced her overly active hormones to take a backseat and tried to say something, but all she could do was nod.

Chapter Nine

When Cam got to Mack's garage, she pulled down a side street and parked. They got out of the car and closed their doors as quietly as they could. There were buildings on both sides of the coastal highway, but in this part of town, only a few were actually in business. Most were empty and boarded up. And at this hour, everything was dark and closed for the night.

Farther down the side street they'd parked on, Val could make out the silhouettes of small beach houses through the incoming darkened fog. They were far enough away that Val wasn't too concerned about anyone noticing them.

Val, however, did feel a bit disconcerted and realized the mood was coming from Cam's reaction to their kiss. It was so odd, like she regretted initiating it. Val would have wagered her entire 401K that Cam liked it as much as she did. Kisses told a more authentic truth than most other methods of communication, and she could have sworn she'd *felt* Cam's truth. But it was like Cam suddenly woke up from a dream and remembered she was late for work or something.

Even though Cam had instigated the whole thing, she decided to let it go. It wouldn't be good for Val to go all psychologist on the situation and try to analyze what the hell was going on.

But, damn, it had felt so good.

They walked around to the front of Mack's, and Val winced, walking as slowly and carefully as she could.

"Are you okay?" Cam said, reaching out to her. "Maybe it's too soon to be out."

"I'm fine," she said. She knew, whether she was lying in bed or walking around, that she'd feel like shit for a while. The aspirin seemed to help, though.

Every so often, a car or truck would drive past on the dark Coast Highway, and Val and Cam would stand still until the silence of the night took over again.

Val made her way over to the front door and peered in through the glass. The darkened waiting room was empty so she pulled on the knob, but Cam's hand was right there to stop her.

Cam pointed. "The office and waiting room are alarmed, see?"

An electronic eye blinked like a small cyclops that hovered up in the corner, watching them.

"I don't think the garage itself is wired. His office has the cash register, and it's a well-known fact that he takes his money with him every night."

"Then why would he alarm the office?"

Cam blinked as she realized the same thing. It didn't make sense at all.

They heard the rumble of a truck approaching so they moved down the side of the building until they were in shadow. The eighteen-wheeler passed by and boomed down the road, switching gears as if clearing its throat a couple times.

"Look," Cam said as she pointed into the windows of the garage area. "See that tool shed? That's locked up like Fort Knox, but otherwise, the rest of the place is clear of alarms."

Val surveyed the room, looking for other red eyes, but found none. "The bay doors are locked up pretty well, but maybe there's a better way in out back. Let's go look."

A back alley served the garage. It was made of hard-packed sand, and their shoes crunched so loudly they were forced to take slow, quieter steps, just in case.

"There," Val pointed, "Mack took us out to that shed when I was here last. We came out that door." She swung her arm toward a wooden door that sat crooked on its hinges.

Cam pulled on the ceramic doorknob. The rickety door yielded a little, and paint chips that had held on for decades broke off and floated to the ground, but it didn't give way.

Cam backed up. "All it needs is a good kick."

Val reached up and grabbed her arm. "Look."

"Where?"

"Past the shed. That's the girl's car! The one that hit the deer first!"

They went over to it, but Val let Cam get a few steps ahead. When Cam bent over to examine the front, Val grimaced in anticipation. "Are there deer guts all over it?"

Cam didn't answer right away. Val watched as she clicked on her cell-phone flashlight app and bent over to inspect the grill. When she got down on her knees to peer under the frame, Val's arousal flared, and pictures of Cam in that same position, but in bed, made Val moan under her breath. She was unbelievably hot and sexy. Those strong arms and legs and beautiful mouth were made for pleasing women.

And she probably doesn't like me that way, Val thought. It was probably for the best. Cam had an illicit past that Val couldn't prove had remained there.

Cam banged on something, and Val wondered if she'd found deer parts under there. "Poor thing…I hope it didn't feel much."

"It didn't feel anything," Cam said.

Val craned her neck and took a step forward. "That's good."

Cam stood and turned to her. "It didn't feel anything because a deer didn't hit this car."

"What do you mean?"

"Are you sure this is the same car?"

"Yes…I mean, how many Buicks are there in Hemlock?"

Cam's expression turned sardonic. "Take a better look. Tell me if you think this is the same Buick."

Val looked it over and thought a moment. She slowly ambled over to the back of the car.

"Yes. This is it." She pointed to the bumper, and Cam came around to flash her light on it. "'Land your Bow at Dory Cove Restaurant.' That's the same bumper sticker."

"Well, I can tell you that this car did not hit a deer. Come here." At the front of the car, Cam said, "Look. See this grill and hood? It's obvious that Mack hasn't started repairing it. There's not enough damage for a deer hit. These dents and dings are rusty and old."

"Cam, I know I hit a deer."

"I don't doubt you. All I'm saying is that a deer would have had to leap over this car to cause such little damage here."

"Can they do that?"

Cam laughed. "No! I was just kidding. This car was hit by a hammer or something else metal. Not a deer."

"I just about had a deer sandwich that night. It came so close to me I could see its fur."

Val watched Cam as she walked around the car. She was deep in thought, and Val liked the way she studied everything with such command. When Cam reached the front of the car again, she ran her hands under the hood, feeling for something. Val heard a clacking sound, and then Cam lifted the hood.

"This latch is broken."

She locked the hood in an upright position and inspected the engine. She then turned her attention to the underside. Rubbing her finger on something, she told Val to come closer and hold her cell phone up.

"See this," Cam said, "these tiny holes? Now look here."

Directly below, on the body of the car right next to the hood latch, were matching holes.

"Someone drilled these recently." She flicked at the holes with her finger.

"What are they for?"

"I have no idea, but they're unusual."

In the dark, Cam's eyes looked inviting and Val knew she was being silly, but her body hadn't been acting very appropriately since she'd watched Cam get down on her knees.

"Are you okay?" Cam was looking at her oddly.

"Yes. I am. Fine. Thank you."

Cam paused, and Val hoped she wouldn't pry.

"Okay," Cam said. "We need to go look at your car."

They walked back over to the door. Cam tried it again, pulling on the doorknob. It shook but still wouldn't open.

"It won't take much to push the door open," Val said.

Cam looked up and down the alley. "Are you sure you want to do this?"

"Something really weird is going on, and I'd rather not get gassed or beaten up again."

Cam paused, then said, "You go to the corner of the building. We'll wait until a big truck goes by. Signal me when it's right out front, and I'll kick the door."

Val hesitated, but not because she thought she might get caught. She stepped closer to Cam.

"Donna told me she thought it was probably you that had been searching through my things. She told me I should stay away from you."

"Me?" Cam said. "Do you think I have something to do with this?"

"I admit that I'm very confused. I really don't know what to think. But something told me to call you instead of asking her for help."

"And here I thought it was my heavenly turtles."

"Seriously, I think I should be asking you the same question. Are you sure you want to do this? If you get caught…"

"We're not here to steal anything. We're just going to take a look. Plus, I want to do this. I know Mack's a fucking asshole, but if he's committing a crime, he needs to be caught. If we can find anything you can take to the police," she said and pointed to the door, "then we'll figure out how to explain this."

"You're not over Donna, are you?"

Cam paused, and Val felt the strange twinge of envy.

"I'm asking because I know you really don't like Mack and I wondered if…" Val hesitated because the question suddenly felt meddlesome.

"I'm not over what she did to me." Cam reached up and put her hand around Val's arm. "There's a difference."

"Are you seeking retribution, maybe?"

"As much as you're seeking the truth."

Val smiled, although she still felt like she was the outsider. But what stake did she have in Cam? None, really. They'd kissed once.

Val hadn't been able to read the look on her face. Maybe she hadn't been exactly bowled over. Plus, Cam had a world of history with Donna, Mack, and this town. Val was just an interloper watching a ship that Cam and Donna had once sailed together and was now crashed on the rocks.

And it was possible that their boat was just stuck, waiting to be saved and relaunched.

Maybe that was what was behind Cam's need for retribution. She certainly seemed to have a different reason for wanting to open that rickety old door. Was Cam simply trying to help Val figure out what was happening to her? Was she involved in some disturbing Hemlock plot in which Val was the mark? Or, Val worried, was Cam trying to find something about Mack that would have Donna running back to her arms?

She stepped away and walked to the corner of the building that looked south on Pacific Coast Highway. It was dark, but in the spots of moonlight that shone through the evergreens, she could see a low-rolling layer of fog coming in from the ocean, creeping across the asphalt of the road like an overflowing bathtub spreads water over a bathroom floor.

She looked back and saw Cam watching her, ready to react.

Should she trust her? Not much was making any sense since she'd arrived in Hemlock. Granted, she'd been the one to walk into Cam's store, so apparently whoever had cracked her on the head earlier hadn't planned their meeting.

Maybe she was making a big deal about everything. Two events didn't necessarily add up to a coincidence.

It was very quiet out. The wind rustled trees here and there, and the only other sound came from a bird far off somewhere toward the water. She was pretty sure it was a storm petrel, a gray seabird with white tail feathers and britches. One of her middle-school teachers had once said their sound was like a cat purring, but to Val, it was more like the rapid chirping of a squirrel, with inconsistent high and low chirps. Some lived to be thirty years old. Maybe the one she heard had been around when she last lived in Hemlock. Like Cam, and Donna and Mack, maybe the storm petrel had stayed here and been shaped and formed by the little town by the sea, with the same amount of paradox and contradiction as its purring or chirping.

A low rumble came from the north. She couldn't see around the building that far, but she knew a truck was coming. She turned back to Cam and raised her arm. Cam nodded that she was ready.

The sound of a big truck grew, and when she could see the long beam of its headlights on the road, she waited another beat and then snapped her arm down.

The truck roared by, swirling up the fog until its wisps were vaporized.

Val turned and half trotted, half limped back to Cam, who stood there with the door hanging from the top hinge. Cam raised a finger to her ear, and Val understood to listen for the beeping of any pre-alarm.

When no sound came, Cam pushed the door farther inward and they climbed through.

Though the front of the building was made up of windowed sliding garage doors, there wasn't enough light from the street to help them see much. Val took the lead, tiptoeing carefully toward where she'd last seen her car. Her heart was racing, and she felt as well as heard the *glug glug* of its pulsing in her ears.

"There," she whispered. "Those are the parts Mack took off my mom's car."

They bent down and studied the grill and hood.

Cam ran her hands over the grill. After a minute, she said, "This is a deer hit."

Val moved closer and Cam took her hand, guiding it along the grill.

"How can you tell?"

"There's blood and flesh here…and here."

Val pulled away quickly. "Ugh! Okay." She stood. "See? It was a deer."

"Shit," Cam said.

Val's adrenaline was surging through every part of her body, and suddenly, she realized she had to pee.

"I'll be right back."

"Where are you going?"

"Bathroom. It's right there." She gestured to the door, and as she tiptoed over to it, Cam whispered rather loudly.

"Hurry up!"

Val carefully closed the door, pushing it until it clicked. She turned the light on, and the whirring sound she'd heard the first time she used the bathroom started again. She hastened to the toilet and dropped her pants. Hovering over the toilet and holding her ribs, she was still puzzled. She looked up and realized the noise was coming from a fan on the ceiling above her. Relieved, she finished her business and zipped up, but paused. She flushed and climbed onto the toilet. The noise was coming from the fan, but the fan blades weren't moving. As a matter of fact, she could see through the grill that the fan blades had been removed from the mechanism. She reached up to the grill and pulled, but it was screwed on tight.

Flipping her cell phone on, she pecked at the flashlight app and pointed the light up.

Her mouth opened suddenly. "Fuck."

There, beyond the grill and pointing down, was a small video camera. Its red indicator light had been taped over. She now knew that the whirring noise meant that it was turned on, recording her.

She backed away and almost fell off the toilet. She yelped at the muscles that were bruised and painful, and scrambled down. She got to the door and flung it open so hard that Cam yelped, "Geezus!" from the other side of the garage.

"Cam! Come here, now!" Val was frantic, feeling the need to run as far away as possible, but it was too late.

"What?" Cam was at her side and Val grabbed her arm, pulling her back into the bathroom.

Val stopped at the doorway and put a finger up to her lips. She turned the light off. The whirring stopped. She turned it back on and the whirring began again.

"It's the fan," Cam said.

Val flicked the switch once more. "It's off now, come here."

Standing by the toilet, she turned her cell-phone light upward. Cam squinted and then climbed on top of the toilet seat. And a second later, Cam turned around and looked down at Val.

"Holy shit."

Cam got off the toilet and they moved away. "That bastard is taping whoever comes in here."

"Jesus."

"I heard that noise the other day and couldn't figure it out."

Cam shook her head. "I don't think Donna's gonna like the fact that Mack's taping all the housewives pulling their pants down."

Val pulled Cam out of the bathroom.

Cam stopped just outside the door. "That sick fuck. We need to go to the police."

"I'm on the tape, Cam. If we go to the police, it'll be obvious that we broke in."

"Well, we need to get the tape either way, because Mack's going to find out you broke in."

Cam went back in, and Val leaned against the open door. She watched Cam climb up onto the toilet and pull at the grill.

"I tried that. Let me go get a screwdriver." Val hurried off to the garage and found one.

In less than a minute, the grill was off and Cam pulled the camera out.

"Shit."

"What?"

"It's hardwired. This is just a camera. The recorder's somewhere else."

"It's gotta be in Mack's office."

But as soon as Val said that, she could tell that Cam realized what she'd just remembered. "His office is alarmed."

"We can still go to the police with this," Cam said as she stuffed the camera back up and screwed the grill back in. "You can say you saw it when you were in the bathroom the other day."

Just as Val was about to argue that she was still on the camera, proving she broke in to the garage, a swath of light cut across the back wall of the garage.

They froze, and Val watched the sudden horror in Cam's eyes. A split second later, they ran out of the bathroom. Cam darted ahead of her and Val followed, trying to bend over like Cam was, so no one would see her through the windows.

The engine of whatever car was just outside was still running, so Cam motioned for her to wait and snuck across the garage to the window of one of the bays.

Over the pounding of her heart, Val could barely hear her own breathing, which was rapid and shallow. Soon it wouldn't matter that she was on tape. They were caught.

Cam snuck back, slower this time.

"The car pulled in and turned around. It's leaving now."

"Shit" was all Val could say, but her guts were cussing up a storm.

In the dark, Cam's eyes were large white cue balls. "Let's get the hell out of here."

Val reached the back door, but Cam told her to wait while she picked up a metal piece that was lying on a workbench at the back wall. It was about eight inches long and maybe six inches wide. She turned it over twice before looking up at Val. "Okay, I said we weren't going to steal anything. But I lied."

She trotted over to Val and they made their way outside. Val propped the door back as best she could and Cam took a deep breath, blowing it out loudly.

"I hope it takes Mack a while to figure out his door is broken," Val said as she turned the doorknob to latch it, helping the door appear to be locked, then wiped her hands on her pants.

"The bastard will be too busy watching women pee to notice," Cam said as they walked back down the alley. "As soon as we find out why those people are after you, I want to blow the whistle on Mack's little adult video production."

"Remember, I'm still on it."

They got to the street and headed for Cam's car. Val held her ribs again, and Cam gently placed her arm around her. "We'll have to figure out something to fix that."

Though she knew Cam was referring to the video, she wished she were talking about Val's ribs. She let Cam's embrace mean that Cam was taking care of her and Cam would fuss over her injuries. It was a fantasy, sure, but she liked the little thrill it gave her.

CHAPTER TEN

It was just after two o'clock in the morning, and Val was sitting on her couch looking at a small plastic medicine bottle while Cam sat next to her examining the metal plate. She turned it over, examined it, and turned it over again. She took a pen from the coffee table and began poking at the screw holes.

Val's muscles had finally calmed down. "The Vicodin is helping a lot more than the aspirin."

Cam's laugh was sweet. "That's because it's a controlled substance and it kicks ass."

She shook the pill bottle. "It says my mom had back pain."

"How many are left?"

"Four."

"That should get you through the worst part. But be careful. Those things are addictive."

"How long do you think it'll take Mack to check his video tape?" Val put the bottle in her pocket.

"I hope longer than it takes us to figure out what those thugs were looking for."

The Vicodin helped her pain, but anxiety still broke through, piquing her worry. And on top of all that, her gut felt sick about her old friend Donna. "Do you think she knows Mack's videotaping women in his bathroom?"

"I doubt it." Cam placed her hand on Val's thigh. "But people change sometimes."

Val considered her response, but it was hard to with Cam's warm hand on her leg. It felt comforting. She wasn't sure she should totally trust the feelings, but at the moment, she was spent from their recent criminal activities and fatigue was setting in. At least that's what she told herself.

"I take it not for the better."

"No."

"Do you speak from experience?"

Cam bit her lower lip in a way that was so endearing.

Val nudged her with her shoulder. "Tell me about Donna."

"The Donna I was with," Cam said, "was sweet, nice. We had a great first two years. Then..." Cam looked up toward a painting on her wall, but Val wondered if she was actually peering into the past. "Then she started to change. She refused to be close. Refused to have sex." Cam shrugged, but the act of indifference didn't seem sincere. "I know those things happen after a while, but this was different. She'd cringe when I touched her."

"Why, do you think?"

"I didn't know at first. Then I found out she was sleeping with Mack. When I confronted her, she couldn't have cared less. By then she'd already started changing. She started keeping strange hours and dressing like she was a biker chick or something."

"I saw her in a leather outfit the other day."

"That's what I mean. By the time we broke up, she was no longer the Donna I knew."

Val could see that she looked a little hesitant to elaborate.

"I noticed a lot of little things. She bought a new purse that was, like, S&M themed, and she began wearing a lot of makeup. But the most telling of all was that she changed all her computer passwords and never let her cell phone out of her sight. She even took it with her into the shower."

Cam moved her hand back to the piece of metal, and Val felt a twinge of disappointment.

"The coffee's got to be ready," Val said, getting up and going to the kitchen. "Do you take cream and sugar?"

She heard Cam call from the living room. "I own a candy store. What do you think?"

Val smiled as she prepared the mugs.

"You know," Cam said, "you should probably see if your mother has an extra set of keys for the house and the car."

"Yeah. I don't want to keep leaving the house unlocked. I mean, these people could come back anytime, but if they haven't found what they're looking for yet, maybe they'll start looking somewhere else."

She paused, then opened the utility drawer. Rummaging around, she felt the quick ignition of frustration.

"Where would she keep a key?"

"What?"

Val found a package of chocolate-chip cookies in a cabinet. She held it under her arm, returned to Cam, and handed her a mug.

"I'm just trying to figure out where my mom would have kept an extra set of keys. It'd make sense that she'd keep them in the kitchen utility drawer. But then again, my mom wasn't used to doing things the ordinary way."

She opened the cookies and offered one to Cam.

"You could call a locksmith and have the door locks changed," Cam said as she bit into the cookie. "And I'm sure an auto dealer would get you a new car key."

"Yeah, I'd better do that tomorrow." Val chewed on a cookie. "It just bothers me that I can't figure out what they want."

"Did your mom ever say anything about people breaking into her home? Had this happened to her before?"

"No. She never mentioned anything about that."

Cam nodded. "Did she have expensive jewelry? Or something else of value?"

"No. She wasn't a flashy person."

Drinking a sip of her coffee, Cam focused on something across the room, maybe a speck on the wall or something, and Val watched her. It seemed so strange that they barely knew each other in high school, and, if they were still there, she probably wouldn't even be hanging out with her. Granted, they were older now and, Val liked to think, possibly more mature.

And where Cam had said Donna changed for the worse, Val liked to think that Cam had accomplished quite the opposite. She'd endured a rough childhood, and while it had to have been really difficult, she eventually became an adult and even started her own business.

"When we were talking before, you said you couldn't leave Hemlock. Why was that?"

Val waited during Cam's silence, not knowing if the truth was bad news or just too private.

"I had two reasons, actually." Cam fidgeted a little. "I was arrested."

"For what?"

"Vandalism."

"What happened?"

"Let's just say that one night some cement blocks came in contact with six windows at the high school."

"When was this?"

"I was nineteen. It was all really stupid. I sat in jail for three months. And as you can probably imagine, when I got out, the town was even more accepting of me than before."

"What was the other reason?"

"I had to stay until I paid for the damage. I was living on my own, so it was pretty hard and took three years. By the time I paid it all off, I just didn't have any motivation to leave. People knew me, which was bad, but then again, they knew me, which helped. A little. Plus I had no car and no plans. College was never a possibility, so I just stayed and worked wherever I could."

Cam lifted the mug of coffee to her lips. "But you got out."

"I did."

"Dallas, you said?"

"Yes."

"Do you miss the ocean?"

Val smiled. "I really do. Mostly the cool, salty air and the smell of pines."

"And growing up here? How was that?"

"Normal, I guess. My mom had been single since my dad left. That was when I was two."

"Did you ever see him again?"

"No. Have no idea where he is. Mom had a lot of boyfriends, though. I didn't like any of them. I was in the way. And Mom usually chose them over me. I guess I can't blame her because at least what little money they made paid for their beer. She had a crappy job. Anyway, about five years ago, she kicked the last one out for good. She got by on social security, though it wasn't much. I'd send her money when I could, just a little, though. That's why I can't understand what the heck people could want from her. Everybody knows she wasn't rich."

Cam nodded. "I knew your mom was a nice lady. Beyond that, I knew she wasn't rich, but then again, few people in this town are." Cam pulled out another cookie from the bag and bit into it. "Mmm, this cookie's great. You're a fantastic baker."

"Why, thank you. I also package them myself."

"I should consider hiring you at the shop."

Val froze as a distant memory suddenly snapped into her mind.

"That's it!" She jumped up so fast, Cam almost spilled her coffee in surprise. "Ow ow ow," she said, her ribs stinging.

"Do you need a job that badly?"

"No." She pointed to the photo album, still opened to a picture of her mother and her posing as if they were chefs. "My mom wasn't a baker!"

"What are you talking about?"

"Come here," Val said as she headed for the kitchen.

Cam followed her and watched as Val opened the tall cabinet door next to the refrigerator, pulling out a large glass container.

"She wasn't a baker. She hated the science of it. Too complicated, she said."

"Yeah, I get it. She preferred store-bought cookies."

"No, that's not it." Val carried the container back out to the dining room.

Placing it on the table, she said, "This is flour. But she didn't *bake*."

"Okay…"

"So why did she have so much flour?" Val picked up the container. "I'll show you."

She turned the jar sideways and thrust it out over the table. The flour came flying out, dumping a mini mountain onto the tabletop.

"What are you doing?"

Flour went everywhere, skidding across the table and out over the edges like clouds escaping over an ocean cliff.

Val put the container down and dug her hands into the mess. She fished around and suddenly pulled her hands out. They were caked in white powder, but one held a key.

"Shit!" Cam almost laughed, her face brightened in apparent amusement.

"She hid things in the flour. That was the only reason she had it. She said no burglar would ever look for valuables in the kitchen, let alone in a jar of flour."

"I need to remember that trick," Cam said, and held out her hand.

Val dropped the key into it. "If this is what they're looking for, it makes sense that they took my other keys."

"The only problem," Cam said, examining the key, "is this doesn't look like it goes to a car or a house."

She held it up. Cam was right; it was too small for either.

"Well, what the heck does it unlock?"

"Good damn question. But it's obviously important in some way. Otherwise she wouldn't have hidden it."

"Let me see it," Val said. "It's a Master key. Here." She pointed to the logo stamped into the nickel silver.

"Could it be to a shed? Or some lock box in the garage?"

"No shed and no locked boxes. I've been through every square inch of this place. This doesn't go to anything here."

As Val brushed a strand of hair from her face, Cam reached up and brushed some flour off her cheek.

"You were pretty forceful spilling out that jar."

Her touch surprised Val, and her hopes jumped around inside her. Cam looked at her, and Val thought she saw a spark of interest. Her eyes were bright and her smile seemed playful.

"What can I say, I was caught up in the moment."

"So what do you think the key goes to?"

The moment drifted away, but Val stayed with it until Cam spoke again.

"What about a bank safe-deposit box?"

"No, I have…had that. It was on the keychain. And those are long and have special numbers." She held up the key. "This is your average garden-variety—"

Val stopped mid-sentence. A thought was forming and she frowned, forcing it to come forward. And when it did, she said, "Oh, shit. That's it!"

She walked back to the coffee table and picked up one of the photo albums. Opening it, she found what she was looking for and turned it around for Cam to see.

Cam leaned in. "This was the play your mom was in last year. *The Girls of the Garden Club*."

"And this is your average garden-variety key."

"I don't get it."

Val stood. "You will. What are you doing tomorrow night?"

Chapter Eleven

The Hemlock Community Theater was located toward the southern part of town. Its exterior walls, with no windows, wore patches of paint that probably used to be dark green but now appeared more as if lichen had attached itself in spotty places to the red bricks. The theater's marquee poked out just far enough that passersby on Coast Highway might be tempted to stop; however, it looked like two of the three inner bulbs had burned out long ago, leaving the translucent plastic and black Helvetica letters looking a little dull.

Cam and Val pulled up to the curb about fifty feet away because the ten-car parking lot was full, as were most of the overflow spots up and down the highway.

Val checked her watch. "The play should be over soon."

"How are you feeling?" Cam asked.

"Better today. The Vicodin is helping. I can walk without wincing, and I found out that my head is thicker than I thought."

"Is that something I should worry about?"

"My injury or my stubbornness?"

"Both."

"Naw. I'm fairly harmless."

"I'm not so sure about that."

Val liked Cam's kidding around. It was a little flirtatious and encouraging.

She reached for her door latch. "Ready?"

"Let's go."

The box-office window was unmanned so they went inside.

A musty smell greeted Val as they walked in, and while it might turn off some, the sensation that hit Val's nose spoke of happy times filled with costumes, food, old carpet, and smoke. The floors creaked like little tattletales as they walked toward a set of double doors.

Projected voices and scattered laughter greeted them as they slowly opened the doors and tiptoed in. They found a place just inside and below the tech booth to stand.

The play looked delightful as the amateur actors cavorted about, some overemphasizing their lines of dialogue and others laying on the body language.

A big, burly man in jeans and a tight T-shirt stood off to the side, and Val motioned for Cam to take notice. When he turned and saw them, his ensuing effeminate walk toward them was significantly juxtaposed to his brawny, masculine style.

"It's almost over, ladies," he whispered. "The next showing will be tomorrow night."

"I'm Val Montague."

The man's eyes brightened and he immediately hugged her.

"My Lord! You're Val!" He was still whispering. "Your mother talked about you constantly! She was so proud of you down there in Dallas. I'm Phil Drago. I own the place. Oh, I'm so glad to finally meet you."

At once, it seemed like a sharp pain passed across his face because his cheeks tightened and his eyebrows crinkled.

"I'm so sorry about your mother. We all miss her terribly. Kris was a fantastic woman, and it was so sudden. One day she was here just working away, and the next..." Only a flick of his hand indicated that he had finished his sentence.

Val stepped back and said, "This is Cam Nelson."

"I know who you are. You're supposed to be a renegade, but all I know is your turtles are so heavenly, you just can't be all that folks say."

"Thank you. I think."

"Oh, I'm an old queen, honey, and I never mince words. You're not the only one whose picture is listed in the town dictionary under pariah." He leaned toward her as if telling a secret. "Admittedly, yours and mine are the only pictures, but at least we're in print."

Cam smiled. "It's very nice to meet a fellow scoundrel."

"Flattery will get you anywhere." He chuckled. "So how long are you here, Val? Will you come see the play? Please do. Your mother was the prop master. Did you know that?"

"Yes, I did. I know you're in the middle of a run, but I was hoping that after the play I could look at the props. I won't take anything. It's just that some of them were my mother's, and I wanted to see if there was anything I needed after the play ends."

"That was your mother all right! Most of the props are hers! Our budgets are so low we can't afford to buy anything." He laughed as quietly as he could. "She was so generous. She would have brought half her house over here if we had the room.

"Of course you may look through anything you see. When everyone has cleared out of the auditorium, please go in. I'll be in the box office counting receipts. Just let me know when you're leaving."

"Do come and see the play," he said as he hugged her again. "Lord, I miss Kris so."

"I will."

❖

The audience began clapping, signaling that the play had ended. The actors coming out from backstage joined the ones onstage, and they all took a bow together. Val guessed the theater held forty or fifty people, so it didn't take long for the crowd to file out of their rows of wooden seats.

A few stragglers chatted with the actors, but the stage was empty so Val and Cam took the few steps leading up from the audience area.

This had been where Mom found so much enjoyment, Val thought. The theater and the church had pretty much made up her life. As she looked around, she recognized many of the pieces of set dressing.

The picture that hung on the right side set wall was very familiar. She'd stared at it a million times, wishing that just one of those horses depicted running wild on a mountaintop would somehow break free and come find her so it could live in her backyard.

Val touched Cam's arm. "That used to hang in my room. I got it when I was twelve."

"Girls and their horses."

"I know, right?"

"I wanted one after I saw Tatum O'Neal in *International Velvet*," Cam said.

"You did?"

"Well, maybe it was more about Tatum, but I did want a horse, too."

Val pushed Cam's shoulder, which made her sidestep away toward a bookcase.

"I can't believe Mom kept it."

Val saw Cam smile as they searched the set. She wondered what thoughts were behind the expression as Cam turned to pick up books, flipping through a few. She wanted to ask her, but a niggling of distrust still wormed around in her stomach, feeling a bit discomforting.

At a side table next to the couch at center stage, she studied a plant that sat on a short, doily-covered stand of some kind. She lifted the doily and bent over, circling it to look at all sides, then called to Cam, hooking her head to get her to come over.

"Bingo."

They both gazed at a dark-blue metal box, about six inches square. On the front, but facing away from the audience, was a lock. Val bent down to get a closer look.

"It's a Master lock," she said as she reached into her pocket and pulled out the key. "And this is a Master key."

"Awesome," Cam said.

Val wondered if her own expression was as full of anticipation as Cam's. It seemed so, but she also watched for a twitch or a dubious gleam, any sign that Cam had less altruistic reasons to be glad Val had found it.

Val looked around the room and saw that, by now, everyone else had left. She heard a few voices out in the lobby, but the people speaking sounded too involved to come back in and ask what they were doing.

She held the box in one hand and slid the key into the lock. With a turn to the left, it clicked quietly and she withdrew the key.

The inside of the box was lined with black velvet and contained a folded piece of paper.

She pulled the paper out and opened it.

"It's…some real-estate listings."

Cam looked over her shoulder.

"What the heck?"

Val shook her head, not sure if this was even anything important. She ran her finger down the lines. "There are five addresses." She pointed to the list. "And she wrote this up in the corner."

"October 2nd."

A desolate ache jabbed her heart. "Two days before my mom died."

Cam tentatively placed her hand on Val's shoulder, in the way people reach out when they're not sure they have the right to but want to.

"I'm sorry," Cam said softly, "but is there a connection?"

"I have no idea. Maybe it's nothing."

"But maybe it's something." Cam motioned for her to sit down beside her on the couch.

"Maybe that's what those people are looking for," Val spoke her thoughts out loud, "except they didn't know they were looking for a key. They were looking for what was in the box the key opened. She had the key, and I have to assume that since this paper is dated two days before her death, she put it here, told no one, and buried the key in the flour. But is it a coincidence or was it deliberate?"

"Let's say she put this here for a reason and wanted someone to find it. That someone is obviously you."

"Why should we assume that?"

"If she wanted someone else, she would have told them where the key was. Or made it easier to find. Evidently, whoever was rifling through your house, and maybe your car, had no clue of its whereabouts."

Val held up the paper. "We don't even know if this is what they were looking for."

"What else do we have to go on?" Cam used her hand to chop off points into the palm of her other hand. "Some unknown people, except for the girl from the deer accident, went through your things three different times. Something's really fishy about the accident. Your mom leaves a key that goes to that box, and she puts information in it two days before she…"

Cam's voice dropped off, and Val's natural reaction was to reach over and squeeze her knee. She actually landed a little higher up and was surprised by the feel of her strong thigh. The rapid rush of desire that suddenly surged between her legs caught her off guard. She quickly removed her hand, and the best cover-up was to pretend an itch on her forehead suddenly needed scratching.

Either Cam hadn't noticed or was polite enough not to acknowledge Val's very unsmooth move. "If we only knew why this list was in that box."

Her crotch was still humming so Val cleared her throat, checked to see if her voice might fail her, and attempted to regain some composure.

Cam pointed to the addresses. "Was your mom thinking of buying a new house?"

"I don't think so. Why would she do that?"

"I don't know, but that makes the most sense."

They looked at the list together and Val tried to focus.

Each line had a home address, a seven or eight-digit number after that, and the listing agent's name.

"Okay, so what *do* we know?" Cam's finger tapped the paper. "The listing agent. All of them are Nedra Tobias."

"If she was shopping for a new house, all this means is that Nedra handled every one she's interested in. And if she wasn't in the market, all these houses have something else in common." She thought a moment. "Maybe mom confided in Nedra about something. I mean, they attended the same church so I could see that happening."

Cam made a face that Val couldn't read.

"Unless you just bit into an orange peel, you seem to have had a reaction to what I said."

"All I can say is, Nedra Tobias isn't someone I'd loan money to."

"You don't trust her."

"Not at all. She's a shrewd woman. I know that's what it takes to be a top real-estate agent, but there's something about her I've never liked. She wields a lot of power in Hemlock and owns a lot of property. If my candy shop were closer to the middle of town, she'd find a way to force me to sell. It's happened to a few business people here. I guarantee you that she doesn't drive around town in a bloodred Tesla because she's conscious about the earth's fossil fuels."

"She's the listing agent on my mom's house," Val said. "But to play devil's advocate, if I were picking a real-estate agent, I'd probably go with the one that had the best success rate."

Cam shrugged. "Nedra's probably an okay person. I admit that I'm a little tainted from living in this town all my life."

"I don't blame you. You've been hassled a lot, and it sounds like you've had to fight for everything you have. It doesn't seem that many people in Hemlock ever gave you much of a break."

The lights on the stage suddenly turned off, and the stage became as dark as a coal mine at midnight.

Cam touched her arm and said, "I'll go try to find the switch."

Val followed the sound of her stepping slowly, with a shuffling noise that was only interrupted twice by her knocking into something and mumbling, "Shit."

Cam must have then jumped off the stage because a thump and a grunt came from that direction.

Val waited. The silence was certainly creepy.

"Cam?"

A long time passed while she sat in the dark. She heard some muffled noises that seemed to come from a few different directions and began to get edgy. She didn't like being so vulnerable and exposed. Was some crazy person watching her through night-vision goggles?

Then suddenly, a spotlight popped on, shining a bright tunnel of light that fell upon the set's fireplace. It shut off and another, closer to Val, turned on. She squinted up into the light and then to the seats in front of her.

Val closed the box and set it back on the side table. She replaced the doily and put the key, as well as the paper, in her front pocket. She walked back toward the set wall, calling out to Cam again. A very loud bang came from that direction, behind the wall, and she stopped.

Out of the darkness, a silhouette emerged, and Val threw her hands up, ready to defend herself.

"Hey!" Cam said, "It's just me!"

"You scared the hell out of me! What was that noise?"

"My shin and a chair." She stepped closer. "I'm sorry."

Cam held her shoulders gently. Val took a deep breath, knowing, of course, that the noise had come from Cam, but lately she'd been involved in too many incidents she hadn't been prepared for. She was as jumpy as a Mexican bean in a Southwestern souvenir store.

"Are you all right?" Cam held her shoulders until Val said yes.

"Okay, then. Let's get out of here so we can think."

"Cam," Val said just before they left the theater. "Thanks for backing me in this crazy mess."

Just through the theater's double doors, Val paused in the lobby and turned to Cam.

"I need to say good-bye to Phil. He said he'd be in the box office."

When they looked in the tiny room, it was dark.

"That's strange."

She stood there for a moment.

"Did you see him backstage?"

"No."

Val was perplexed. Would he just leave the building with them still in it? Maybe he trusted her. Maybe he never locked the theater. Maybe she'd never understand small towns.

❖

Cam started her car, which was now the only one left on the street. The road was dark, and only a couple other cars drove down Coast Highway.

"Back to your house?"

Val pulled out the list. "Let's take a drive."

Val searched the houses while Cam idled down Pine Coast Road.

"There. Forty-seven. That's the first house on the list."

Cam stopped in front of the house. There was nothing unusual about it. The shutters were drawn, but a car in the driveway and a dim light in the front room indicated that someone could be home.

"I don't see a for-sale sign in the yard," Cam said. "I wish I knew what we were looking for."

"Me, too." Val glanced back at the house one more time. "Let's go to the next house."

Cam stopped in front of the second place listed. It looked as normal as the first.

Val looked down at the paper and confirmed the address. "217 Hillcrest. This is it."

"Let's see that list." Cam held out her hand.

Val shared it with her, and they almost touched heads reading it together. Cam pointed to the list.

"The third address is about five blocks from here, and the fourth one is right around the corner from here. They're just houses, pretty much like this one." She flicked at the page. "It's this last address that's strange. And it rules out the possibility that your mom was looking to buy a new place."

"How so?"

"It isn't at all like these first four."

Cam started the car.

"Where is it?"

"I'll show you."

In less than five minutes, Cam pulled up to a curb and parked. "Here you go."

"Nedra's selling The Seeds of Light church?"

"No."

"Are you sure?"

"Hell, that would make Hemlock front-page news for weeks."

They sat in silence.

"Something smells."

"I was just here yesterday."

"Why?"

"Donna brought me here. She wanted me to talk to Pastor Kind."

"About your mom's death?"

"I suppose. I mostly just answered his questions."

"That's odd."

"What?"

"Don't they usually answer the questions *we* have?"

Val didn't go to church so she wasn't sure, but it made sense.

"What was he asking you?"

"At the church, he asked me what I was going to do with mom's estate and what we talked about the last time we spoke. Then at my mom's house, he asked me if I saw the attackers and asked what I thought…"

She hesitated, and her heart dropped with remorse.

"What's wrong?"

"I told them you also knew that I was at the motel."

"When you had your things tampered with." Cam understood immediately. "What'd Pastor Kind say to that?"

"He…said he'd tell the police to come talk to you about it. I'm so, so sorry!"

She watched Cam's face for her reaction. The silence between them scared her.

"I think it would be better if I went to the police first."

"You're going to go talk to them?"

"As soon as we find out a little more about what's going on."

Cam started the car, but Val stopped her from shifting by touching her arm. "I didn't know he'd say that when I told him you knew I was at the motel."

"I know." Cam placed her hand over Val's. "It's okay."

"Where are we going?"

"Let's get a bite to eat and regroup."

❖

At a back booth of a restaurant ten miles south of town, a waitress put down two cups of coffee and placed a hamburger in front of Cam. Cam thanked her and gestured to Val.

"Aren't you going to eat anything?"

The waitress paused, looking at her.

"No, thank you," she said to the waitress and watched her walk away. "I'm too confused to be hungry."

"You really should eat."

Val watched her dive into the burger. Cam looked up and smiled.

"One way to get to know someone," Val said, "is to watch them eat."

"What are you finding out about me?"

"You handle stress well."

"It's the red meat."

"Cam, I'm sorry you got involved in this. You were just trying to be nice by coming by the motel, and now the police want to talk to you. Plus, you broke into the garage with me. I know you're already seen around town as a troublemaker."

Cam shrugged as she put the hamburger down. "I've got nothing to hide. Which, I imagine, is more than I can say for my ex."

"I can't believe she's part of this."

"I think you'd better start believing it."

"I can't figure out what's going on. Nedra spends the afternoon in my mom's house and someone goes through my things. I get gassed out of the house, go to a hotel that Donna leads me to, and my things are gone through again. And then you tell me Mack's seeing your ex, who happens to be my ex *and* someone who seems to know more than I thought."

"Don't forget the young girl from the accident who was there when you got attacked."

This was a little too much for Val. All she'd wanted to do was come to town, handle her mom's estate, liquidate the assets, and leave town. She dropped her head to her hands.

"Are you okay?"

"They can't all be involved in this."

"Why not?"

Val looked up. "Nedra Tobias is an old high-society fart. What would she be doing with that girl from the accident?"

Cam nodded, but it didn't seem like she was exactly agreeing. "And why would Donna mention a living trust that she supposedly didn't know about?"

Val sipped her coffee. "If all these unrelated people are actually together on something, the only thing I could guess is that it's for financial gain."

"It makes sense. Nedra fits that bill hands down."

Val pulled the list out of her pocket and flattened it out on the table. She ran her finger over the addresses on the listings.

"All of these places are residences, except for the last one, which is the nondenominational church. So, this isn't a list of possible houses for Mom to buy. But there's something here that Mom needed to hide." She studied the seven-digit numbers on each line. "Maybe these mean something."

"They could just be the multiple-listing codes."

Val took out her cell phone and typed one address and its associated number into Google.

"The number comes up, but it's not this house."

"Try another one."

Val did and she shook her head. "One, zero, zero, eight, nine, three, zero comes up as a residence in Allenspark, Colorado."

"Okay, so it's not an MLS number."

Val stared at the numbers, but her brain couldn't put anything together. "I got nothing." She shook her head slowly. "But we've got to find out what the hell this list means."

"And then we'll go to the police," Cam said. "If they don't find me first."

"Speaking of that, we'd better leave. I know we're way south of town, but what if the police take a dinner break here?"

Cam's eyes widened. "Let's go."

On the way out to Cam's car, she said, "I guess we should assume Mack, Donna, and Nedra know by now that we're together on this, or at least that you've told me about what's been going on."

"That's a safe assumption."

She unlocked the passenger's door for Val. "So they'll be looking for my car."

As Cam walked around to the driver's side and opened the door, Val said, "What should we do?"

They sat down at the same time.

"We need another car."

"We're going to steal a car?"

Cam's laugh was hearty and very cute. Her smile seemed to lighten the atmosphere as naturally as helium lifts a balloon, and a welcoming wave of relief settled over Val.

"No, silly. We're going to borrow one."

As they drove off, Val still wasn't sure what that meant. "Do you mean borrow, as in take without asking and hope to return it before someone finds out?"

Cam laughed again, caressing her hand. "You watch too many TV shows."

"I guess I do."

Cam's warm hand on hers put her at ease, and in the strange and scary saga that was playing out, Val would take whatever comfort she could get. Coming from Cam, those touches also revved up a place of desire inside her that had nothing to do with solving the mystery. Still, she also experienced the uneasiness she would in an airport if someone told her to carry a piece of baggage for them. The smile and touch reassured her, but should she trust them?

Chapter Twelve

Cam parked behind the candy store, and when they got out, reached for her hand. They walked down the back alley and followed the tree line, passing a few streets that intersected with Coast Highway. At a very overgrown sign that looked like Sandpiper Lane, they turned left, toward the ocean.

The air grew colder, and Val knew they were close to the cliffs overlooking the beach. It was dark, but the heady aroma of saltwater and kelp was undeniable.

They stopped at the front door of a little blue house at the end of the street. Like most of the houses in Hemlock, it was worn from time and the salty elements. Voices accompanied by music came from inside, and Val guessed whoever was home had the television on. Cam knocked on the door. They waited a minute or so, and then Cam knocked louder. Finally the door opened, creaking so loudly, Val thought it might take the frame along with it.

An old man with black trousers and a white, short-sleeve T-shirt stood there. "Cam," he said, his voice a bit gravely. "How the hell are you?"

"I'm fine, Mr. Harlin. I hope we didn't wake you."

"Hell, no. I was up watching Charlton Heston. Who's your pretty friend?"

"This is Val, Mr. Harlin."

The old man reached out and shook her hand, drawing her inside. "So very pleased to meet you. Come on in." He turned to Cam as he shut the door. "What the hell are you doing up so late?"

"I need a favor."

They followed Mr. Harlin to the living room, where he headed over to an old, threadbare easy chair that looked custom molded to his body. When he sat, he grunted and motioned for them to sit on the couch. The place was neat and tidy, but full of souvenirs and keepsakes, and Val guessed that most were older than she was. All the religious icons and pictures bathing the room declared loudly the dominant theme of his place. Jesus watched over everything from five different places, but the Virgin Mary surpassed him in prominence; she reigned supreme in three pictures, four statues, and one ashtray.

"How the hell have you been, Cam?" Mr. Harlin said.

"Very well, thank you."

He turned to Val. "Cam, here, makes sure I'm never out of my favorite candy." He picked up a jar next to him, which had the Apostles painted on the outside. He removed the lid and offered Val the contents.

"Necco wafers?"

Val took a few and thanked him, and he swung the jar over to Cam, who reached in and took some, too.

Val couldn't help but glance over Mr. Harlin's head at a picture of an old-world priest offering communion to some villagers. She looked at her wafers and then back to the picture.

"Now, you never answered my question. What the hell are you two doing out at this time of night?"

"I'm in a bit of a jam, Mr. Harlin. If it's okay with you, I'd like to borrow your car for a day or two."

Without hesitation, he said, "It's yours."

He searched the lamp stand right next to him, picked up a few religious magazines, and found his keys underneath. They were on a keychain attached to a small wooden crucifix.

"I hope we're not putting you out."

"Oh, applesauce," Mr. Harlin said as he handed her the keys. "I haven't driven that car much since twenty aught nine. Old Mrs. Hutchinson brings me my groceries once a month. She's real sweet."

"Thank you, Mr. Harlin."

"Think nothing of it." To Val, he said, "Every week, Monday morning, she brings me my Necco wafers. I used to go by the candy store, but it's getting harder and harder to get out and about. The first time I failed to show, she came by to make sure I was all right. Now I get personal deliveries. Sometimes, she comes by for no reason, just to see if I'm okay and to have a chat. Wish to hell my doctor would do that."

"I really appreciate this," Cam said.

"You're a helluva good woman, Cam." Again, he addressed Val. "She's the real McCoy."

Val smiled, hoping she was.

❖

Cam and Val sat in Mr. Harlin's old Grand Torino. Having stopped by a fast-food restaurant, they sat in the parking lot, and Val was devouring a chicken-breast sandwich, fries, and a Coke. Cam had one of Val's napkins and was doodling on it with a pen.

"Thanks for stopping. I guess I was hungry after all."

Cam cowered away from her. "I'm staying over here. The way that sandwich is getting gobbled down, I don't want my limbs or digits anywhere near your mouth."

"Oh, but this is so good. I think all this will give me are zits, but I don't care."

Cam laughed, slouching down in her seat. As she settled back to doodling, Val summarized what she knew.

"Okay. I get into an accident. The girl that was there shows up when I get beaten up in my home, which I'd just returned to after getting gassed out when a valve somehow turned itself on. This is all, of course, after somebody snooped around my mom's house and my motel room. Not to mention Donna, my old best friend, is sleeping with Mack. And we have a list of numbers."

She took a sip of her Coke. "How is this all tied together? It doesn't make any sense."

"Start with a connection that does."

"Like…?"

"Donna knows Mack."

"Donna knows you, too."

Cam stopped drawing and looked over at her. "She does."

She sipped more of her drink, waiting to see if Cam would elaborate. When she didn't, Val wondered whether it was because she was involved somehow or if she might be upset that her comment had been a mild accusation.

"Mack has my car," Val finally said.

Cam tapped the pen on the napkin. "Mack knows the girl."

"The girl was there when those guys were at the house looking for something."

"Nedra was at your house when you figured out someone was looking for something as well."

"And Donna took me to the motel where someone came to look for, I assume, that same damn something." She looked at Cam. "It's gotta be the key."

"To the box that had the real-estate listings."

"Or the box itself. Which, either way, leads back to Nedra." She shook her head in confusion. It was a state that was becoming fairly common and getting very old. "It's a big freaking circle."

"But don't you think that if they were looking for the box, someone would have seen it at the play? Everyone eventually goes to the theater. Virtually the whole community supports it. That, and because the Bijou's one movie a week is the only other entertainment in town."

"Maybe they didn't know about the box. Maybe they didn't know what they were looking for."

"That complicates things. I mean, it's apparent they weren't looking for money or valuables. So they had to have been looking for something else your mother had."

"And another thing," Val said, "Mom was involved in that church for a long time, but she didn't want anyone with me when I scattered her ashes. I'd think she'd want all of her church friends to be there. In the past ten years they had a closer relationship with her than I did."

Silence enveloped them, and the only sound was Val's chewing and the scratch of Cam's pen on the napkin.

Val finished her french fries. "All because I hit a deer and my car ends up at Mack's." As she licked her fingers, she noticed that Cam had turned to watch her. She tried to read her expression. Was that concentrated scrutiny actually a sign of interest? Or was Cam trying to figure out just how much Val suspected?

The carousel Val was spinning on changed with each revolution. The gold ring was shiny one minute, glowing with the rising attraction she felt for Cam, and then the next time she came around to it, the ring was sullied and warped and something she was leery of reaching out for.

Could she trust Cam? She'd long ago lost the ability to easily believe in anyone. Her mom had known it, and her exes sure had. She so desperately wanted to find out what the hell was going on, especially if she could have faith in Cam, but she needed to be careful.

"Maybe it's a theft ring," Cam said. "I mean, maybe Nedra's giving Mack addresses so he can rob them. She'd list the times the people would be gone from their houses."

"And the church, too?"

"Yeah." Cam twirled the pen between her fingers. "That's where that hypothesis crumbles."

"Maybe whatever this group is doing had something to do with my mom. But why did Nedra wait for the open house to search my mom's place?" Val stashed the sandwich wrap and empty french-fry bag into the fast-food sack and turned in her seat to face Cam. "While I was arranging to fly out here after mom died, Nedra contacted me and told me they were good church friends and asked if she could do anything for me. I told her I needed to take care of the estate, and Nedra asked about the house. I told her I'd sell it, and she offered to handle it for me. I let her know where the spare set of keys was hidden, and she said she'd start the process right away." Val paused for effect. "So, why did she wait for the open house? She could have searched the place any time before I even came to town."

"Maybe Nedra's not involved. Whoever needed to get in waited until the open house. That would certainly be less obvious than breaking in."

"That makes sense, but I still can't figure out what they were looking for. Maybe Mack found something while working on my mom's car that gave him the idea to go through the house."

"Or maybe," Cam said, "he already knew what he was looking for and needed to get access to her car."

"I guess that means the deer was in on it, too." Val laughed at her own joke and slapped her knee to accentuate the guffaw, but she noticed Cam wasn't laughing.

"Maybe."

Val was still chuckling. "Maybe what?"

"Maybe the deer was in on it."

"Last I checked, a criminal needs opposing thumbs to steal something."

"What if…" Cam's eyes looked as if they'd just seen a tornado. "What if it was staged?"

"You do know that sounds absurd, don't you? How can you train a deer to jump out of the woods on cue?"

"You can't. But I keep thinking, how come the girl's car has no evidence of a deer hit, when yours is trashed?" Cam sat upright. "You said it came flying over her hood, remember?" She turned her napkin toward Val and showed her a drawing of the metal plate she'd taken from Mack's garage. She used her pen to point. "Holes were drilled into the engine compartment of the girl's Buick. This metal plate has the same hole placements as the ones on the Buick. I picked it up because it looked out of place in an auto garage. I couldn't figure out why. Then I noticed that one side of the metal plate had a wear mark in it."

Cam drew something while Val leaned closer. "A circle, like this."

"What made the circle?"

"I don't know. But this piece was attached to the Buick, and it's not a regular part of the car. It was jerry-rigged on and then taken off at some point."

"So you believe this plate had something to do with the deer accident."

"Yes. I haven't figured it all out yet, but I'm going to."

A rush of apprehension raced up Val's spine and grabbed her by the throat. When she spoke, her voice came out as a strained whisper. "We're not going back there!"

"We have to, Val. We're this close to figuring it out, and I'd rather take this to the police with an answer than get picked up and grilled without knowing what the hell's going on." She checked her watch. "It's eleven o'clock so no one should be there."

Val sighed and reached up to her forehead. Her hand found the bandaged wound where the men that had attacked her had hit her. She winced a little, but the pain reminded her that something really bad was going on in Hemlock.

"Shit," she said. In for a pound. "Let's go."

Cam and Val pulled up in Mr. Harlin's car and slowed as they passed Mack's garage. They parked on the side street in about the same place they had before. It was close enough to the garage but far enough away to avoid drawing any attention to them. They opened their car doors, and Cam reached up to turn the interior light off.

"Old habit from my ruffian days," she said and shrugged.

They reached the alley and Cam walked alongside Val, who was tamping down a sudden eruption of anxiety in her gut. Thankfully, another Vicodin was streaming around in her blood vessels, and though she still hurt all over, the pain hardly slowed her down. But she wished she had something stronger in her system, like a Valium, because she was as jumpy as a kid in a bounce house.

At this time last week, when she was arranging the flight to Oregon, she would have ranked the probability that her life would be threatened at exactly zero percent. Now, she was planning to break into a business. For the second time. The almost painful pounding of her heart against her breastbone indicated that she was definitely not cut out for this type of excitement.

She was about to raise the possibility that they forget all about this idea when Cam put her arm around her.

"Are you okay?" Cam looked as anxious as she felt.

"I was just wondering if I combed my hair today, in case I have to pose for my first mug shot."

Cam stopped her by the girl's Buick. "We can leave now and forget about this."

"Could you really?"

"My reputation's already ruined, but you have a chance to stay out of trouble."

"I'm already in trouble. It found me, and I don't think I can run away from it."

"Are you sure?"

Val wasn't, at all, but she also couldn't leave Hemlock with so many questions unanswered.

Cam pulled up the Buick's hood and inspected the holes on the underside again. She then looked closely at the car's body, right by the hood latch. The light from her cell phone created a surreal bubble of unnatural light around Cam's face. Val turned it around in her mind and imagined the light coming from a campfire in some romantic national forest while they made s'mores and watched the stars cross the nighttime sky.

Just when Val pictured Cam about to lick melted marshmallow off her lips, Cam said, "See these tiny holes by the hood latch?"

Val blinked into the harsh white light from the cell phone. "What?"

"Here, right above those holes. See these holes on the top of the engine compartment?"

Val leaned forward. "Yes."

"Something was bolted to the inside of the hood."

"That metal plate you found."

"Exactly. And it was done recently. You can see the fresh screw marks. The grime from the engine and road dirt hasn't had a chance to gather."

"What was it used for?"

Cam looked around her. “I’m not sure. There’s no engine part that would logically be connected here. It’s nowhere near the other engine components.”

Cam stepped away and searched around the ground by the car.

“What are you looking for?”

Cam didn’t answer but continued looking. When she found nothing, she nodded toward the back door by the back shed. Val followed her. Cam pulled at the knob, but it didn’t move. “They’ve repaired this,” she said pulling again, “and it looks like they reinforced it, too. Shit.”

“We need to get inside to find out what made those circular marks on that plate.” Val began to survey the rest of the building, walking toward the north end. “All I wanted to do was bury my mom and settle her estate. Now someone has tried to gas me to death and beat me up, and I don’t know why. But what really pisses me off is that I have absolutely no burglary skills to exploit tonight.”

Cam laughed and caught up to her. “Seriously, would you rather go to the police?”

“No! I need to get inside. I’m just scared as shit, that’s all.”

Cam grabbed her in a bear hug. “So am I.”

Val felt the closeness of Cam’s body and closed her eyes. She smelled the clean, almost fruity fragrance of her hair and inhaled deeply. The first twinges of desire shuddered in her stomach, demanding her attention. But an inkling of doubt floated around in her gut. Cam had been a little distant when they’d kissed, and Val didn’t know what the impetus was.

Cam whispered in her ear, “I’m not going to let anything happen to you.”

Pulling away, Val smiled, but the conflict about Cam’s true intentions teeter-tottered inside her. If Cam weren’t sincere in helping her, the truth would be coming out soon. She just didn’t know when and in what form. Her stomach tensed up as if she were anticipating a punch. She turned toward the back door but Cam pulled at her sleeve.

“Aren’t you supposed to say something now?”

“Ahhh. Thank you?”

"No." Cam almost laughed. "You're supposed to tell me that you're not going to let anything happen to me, either."

The muscles in her stomach relaxed a little. "I've got your back," she said. Unless you betray me, she added silently.

"Here," Cam said. "This window. That's how we're going to get in."

It was low enough that they could climb in without jumping. Cam found an old pipe and, as Val turned away, she hit the glass. The sound wasn't like the loud crash Val had heard on TV or the movies. It was more like a dull whop and then a crack as a spiderweb of fractures shot out in all directions. Cam tapped the window and a number of shards gave way, falling inside the shop and onto the ground by their feet.

Cam wiped the pipe with her shirt and dropped it. Right before she crawled through the window, she said, "Don't touch anything and leave a print."

Oh fuck, Val thought as a bullet of dread shot though her. Was Cam practiced at breaking and entering?

CHAPTER THIRTEEN

They stood in silence, and Val strained to hear any noises that might indicate they weren't alone. Just like the last time, the garage was silent; though that night, Val thought it felt spookier.

Cam made a circle by curling her finger and thumb. She was reminding Val about the size of the circle made in the metal plate. Val nodded and they separated to search.

She scanned everything she saw as quickly as she could. She didn't want to stay in the garage a second longer than she had to.

When headlights flashed through the front windows and across the back wall, they froze and waited to make sure the vehicles passed by outside. Each time they resumed their hunt, Val's anxiety rose a little more. With every car or truck, her pulse shot higher, as if a large mallet was smacking the lead puck on a carnival strength-tester. Her nerves were rising higher and higher, getting way too close to the bell at the top. She imagined that if she heard that loud ding, a cardiac arrest was next.

Cam was examining the tool crib, and Val walked over to the back wall of the garage to pick through a pile of parts that sat in a milk crate. All at once she stopped and reached in.

She turned to Cam. "Pssst."

She came over and Val handed her a large spring. It was new and had broken weld marks at each end.

Cam seemed to be as cautious as she was, whispering, "Two and a half inches in diameter. This could be it."

Val opened her palm and Cam handed it back to her. She held it horizontally to push the two ends together, like an accordion. But when she tried, it barely budged. It was so strong she could only compress the spring about a half an inch. She squatted down and stood the spring upright on the concrete floor. Using her full weight, she pushed the spring down, wincing a bit as her ribs protested, and had much better luck. She let go and the force of its expansion made it jump into the air. Val fell backward, landing on her butt, as it dropped back down and clanged onto the floor.

"Shit!" Cam yelped before grabbing the spring.

They both froze in panic again.

Val waited for the bell to ding and the heart attack to begin. When she didn't keel over, she looked at Cam. "That's what the girl's hood did."

"What?"

"When the deer hit it, it sprung open, like this." She pivoted her arm 45 degrees to demonstrate.

"Well, fuck a duck. That's it."

"That girl didn't hit the deer." She took the spring from her. "This was rigged to the metal plate we found. The metal plate was attached to the girl's car, as evident from the new screw holes we saw. Her hood latch is broken, but I could tell it wasn't damaged in the accident because there weren't any other marks around that part of the car."

"Which means," Val said, in perfect synch with Cam's thoughts, "the car's hood was rigged to spring open."

"Yes."

Val closed her eyes, recalling the moment of the crash.

The Buick ahead of her swerved and she saw the brake lights through the rain. She grabbed the steering wheel tighter, not knowing what was going on, and the next thing she saw was something flying over the top of the car.

She hit the brakes and skidded on the wet pavement, and then the deer suddenly came into focus, flying through the air, and smashed into her mom's front grill, onto her hood, and into the windshield.

At once, Val opened her eyes, staring at a grease stain on the wall as the vision remained in front of her eyes. "Oh, my God. That girl swerved, making me think she was trying to avoid the deer and attempting to get my attention. She must have released the spring somehow, which made the hood fly open and catapulted the deer over her car."

"Shit." Cam was no longer whispering. "The deer was already on that girl's hood."

Val blinked away the memory and focused on Cam's face. "Is this too crazy? Are we trying too hard to make something fit?"

Cam was shaking her head. "No. It makes sense. That's why her car doesn't look like a deer hit it."

"So she was trying to get me to stop."

"And to get your car in here to search it."

She instinctively reached for her front pants pocket to make sure the key was still there. "That means this was planned. And it means they knew I was coming into town that night. And only one person had that knowledge."

"Nedra."

"Whether they knew what it was or not, the list is what they were looking for. But why did they want it so badly?"

"I don't know, but I think we should get the hell out of here."

Val nodded, and they started back for the window when her eye caught something on one of the mechanic's workbenches. When she peeled off from Cam, she heard, "Where are you going?" in an inflection that rose a few octaves by the end of the sentence.

She got to the bench and her mouth dropped open.

"Oh, *fuck*!"

She held it up for Cam to see. It was a metal plate with the screw holes in it.

Cam's eyes widened.

"And it's got your pen marks on it."

"They've been in your house again."

Jolts of terror shot up Val's back. "Tonight."

Cam waved her arm rapidly, motioning for her to head over to the window.

"We can't go back there," Val said, moving toward her, but she stopped, handed the spring to Cam, and went back to the bench.

"I think it's time we go to the police."

"With what?" Val picked up the metal plate. "A hunk of metal and a story about a deer catapult?"

"Val, they were in your house. More than once."

Val walked back toward Cam. "We have the spring and the plate but not a whole lot—"

Three loud pops sounded, and one of the panes of glass in the front of the garage shattered. Cam and Val instinctively ducked and flung their hands up to cover their heads. In a surreal and frozen second, Val thought, Now that's what glass breaking sounds like in the movies.

Cam grabbed Val's sleeve. "Time to go."

She pulled her toward the window and they scampered through, Cam holding the spring and Val gripping the metal plate. They ran down the back alley toward the street where Mr. Harlin's car was parked. At the back corner of the garage, Cam suddenly skidded to a halt. Val almost slammed up against her. Cam pointed toward the front of the building, and they both slowly peered around the corner. Mack and two other men were coming around from the front. They all had handguns.

Val pulled Cam backward and they took off running back down the alley, past the girl's Buick and toward the street on the opposite side of the garage.

Val's heart was pounding so loudly, she couldn't hear her own footsteps, but she could make out Cam saying, "The woods!"

They hooked a sharp left just as voices began to shout from behind them. Pushing past branches and snapping others that lay on the ground, Val now ran for her life. She didn't have to turn around to know that branches breaking behind them meant that the men were now entering the woods.

Through her panting, Cam said, "Head for that house."

At the edge of the woods was a clearing that led to the residential street behind Mack's garage. But the closest house still seemed too far away.

Cam and Val crashed through the last of the trees and underbrush, reaching the house and dashing around to the front.

"This way."

Val followed Cam to the street and she led them as they ran, bent over, crouching behind the parked cars they passed. They got a couple of houses down before Val grabbed Cam.

They could hear that the men had reached the street. They'd stopped to look for them. Val peered over the car she and Cam were hiding behind. The men were standing on the sidewalk close enough to one of the house's porch lights that they were illuminated just slightly. She couldn't see much of their faces, but she recognized something else.

Val ducked back down. She leaned close to Cam and whispered as quietly as she could, "Mack's with one of the guys who beat me up. The guy with the Dingo boots. I didn't see much, but I could see his boots."

Cam nodded and they both took a peek.

"Dollars to doughnuts," Cam whispered, "that third guy is the one that helped him."

The three men stopped whatever they were discussing and fanned out, leaving the light of the porch.

Val heard "Oh, shit" and wasn't sure if Cam said it or she thought it.

"They can't just shoot us in the middle of the street," Val said.

"Do you want to stick around to see if you're right?"

Cam and Val took inventory of their situation. They were behind the front grill of a van that was about twenty feet from the man with the Dingo boots. They were on the house side of the van, opposite the man. The man with the Dingo boots held a handgun in his right hand and was walking their way. The other two headed away from them, both with handguns drawn.

Dingo Boots reached a car that sat two cars behind Val and Cam. He squatted down and looked under the car to the other side. He then went one car closer to the van.

Val motioned to Cam and then to the van's front wheel. Cam moved quietly over until she was positioned to hide behind it while Val moved behind the back wheel.

Dingo Boots squatted down again and looked under the second car. He stood and slowly moved toward the van. As he crouched down, Val and Cam froze in place. Instead of standing back up right away, he hesitated.

Val held her breath until Dingo Boots straightened back up. In the silence, Val began shaking. Every part of her body screamed at her—leg muscles wanted to break into a run, brain cells flashed lightning bolts warning of imminent death, and her lungs threatened to gather enough wind to shriek out the impending terror she wasn't sure she could escape.

The chewing of boots on the road indicated that he'd pivoted and taken a step. She locked eyes with Cam, and they stared at each other until it was clear which direction he was heading. She didn't have to see the shock in Cam's eyes to know he'd be at her own side of the van in less than three seconds.

It was too late to run. She'd never escape the speed of a bullet. They'd confront each other. She had no choice but to grip the metal plate, her only weapon.

There wasn't enough light for him to cast a shadow so she had to wait, panicked, as the sound of the slow-moving boots grew louder.

It all happened so quickly. Dingo Boots rounded the corner and she heard Cam hiss. As Dingo Boots jerked his head toward Cam, he almost stepped on Val, who sprang from her crouched position and swung the metal plate as if it were a baseball bat and she was going for the outfield bleachers. Val felt as if her ribs were shattering as she cracked him hard on the chin and left cheekbone.

Cam was suddenly by her side and they grabbed Dingo Boots as he fell, assisting him to the ground to try to deaden the noise. He lay there in a heap, not moving. Val stood over him for a second, ready to crack him again if he regained consciousness, but he wasn't going to come around any time soon.

Val peered around the van and saw that Mack and the other man were even farther away, searching the cars and yards. She motioned to Cam, who quickly surveyed their options and pointed to the house that the van was parked in front of.

"Behind." Cam's whisper was strained. "Backyard, to the car."

And they ran.

Just as they reached the house, they heard Mack yell. He'd spotted them. Val followed Cam as she ran behind the house and back into the woods toward Mack's garage. She figured Cam's plan was that Mack would assume they'd run farther away, not back from where they came.

Behind them, Mack yelled, "Stay with him." They'd obviously come upon Dingo Boots. That meant Mack was the only one chasing them.

Val fought her way through the branches and undergrowth, feeling the burning slices and pokes all over her arms and face.

They reached the alley and ran past the back of the garage, getting to the street and somehow over to Mr. Harlin's car without being seen. Cam followed Val to her side of the car, away from the street, and scrambled to unlock the passenger door. They climbed in, thankful Cam had turned the interior light off earlier, and hunkered down, out of view. Val began to hyperventilate and dropped the metal plate on the floorboard by her feet. She grabbed the spring from Cam and flung it down, too. She slid down even farther in the seat, gasping for air and wheezing uncontrollably. Cam reached over to hold her hand, and Val could tell she was shaking.

She watched Cam's other hand tremble as she reached across her lap and into her pocket. She retrieved the car keys, and as she slid them into the ignition, Val stole a peek out the window over Cam's head. Cam was just about to turn the key when Val barely eked out, "Stop!"

Mack was walking down the alley toward them, his gun pivoting as he looked left and right. She removed her hand from the ignition.

Mack now crept up to a pile of boxes stacked against the back of the garage. He took his time searching every potential hiding place.

Headlights flashed and a car turned off Coast Highway, driving right toward them. They slid farther down in their seats, and the inside roof of their car lit up from the headlights. Val watched them swing toward the alley, and they both inched back up again.

A police car. Val inwardly cheered. Help is here!

The officer got out and walked over to Mack. He no longer had the gun and reached out and shook the officer's hand.

Val's heart sank. Help just left.

They watched as Mack gestured toward the inside of the garage and talked.

Cam said, "I can see this one coming. Mack's going to tell the cop we just shot up his garage."

"And then he'll take him over to that guy I hit."

"Guess who he'll suggest did it?"

"They won't have any proof."

After a brief pause between them, Cam turned to Val as they said in unison, "The video camera."

They spoke at the same time again, but when Cam said, "Shit," Val said, "Fuck."

"But he won't show it to him tonight," Val said. "He's gonna have to edit out the kinky parts first."

"If we don't find out what the hell this list is all about, we'll be in deep shit."

"And we're going to have to avoid the police until tomorrow night."

"Not to mention Mack and his goons." Cam checked her watch. "Actually, just until tonight. It's almost one A.M."

They looked back at Mack and the police officer. They talked for a few more minutes, and then Mack shook his hand again.

"He didn't show him the broken window."

Cam was right. "I don't think he said anything about us."

"Fuck. That means he'd rather take care of things himself."

Val looked at her. "That's not good."

The police officer got back into his car and drove off. Mack stood there another beat, and just before he walked back down the alley, he took one last look around.

They watched him retrace their previous path and disappear into the woods.

"He's going back to his buddies."

Cam started the car. "Time to go."

"But where?"

❖

Outside a convenience store, Cam returned to the car with a bag of groceries and two cups of coffee. Val took the bag from her as she got back in.

"Thanks. I got some munchies, a blanket, and a flashlight. Just in case."

"It probably wasn't smart stopping here."

"You're right." Cam started the engine and looked in the rearview mirror. "What's the plan?"

"A hotel is out. The police might decide we're suddenly worth scouring the town for."

"You mean a shot-up garage and a cold-cocked guy is enough to send out the cavalry?"

Cam dropped her head and smirked. "This is Hemlock."

"Let's get out of town."

"Pick a direction."

Val thought a moment. "North." It was much less populated past the Hemlock city limits. And the road was virtually pitch-black in the twenty or so miles to the next town.

CHAPTER FOURTEEN

Cam pulled onto a gravel road at the turnout for Cascade Head Mountain. A U.S. Parks sign announced the entrance to Cascade Head Conservancy. As the car traveled down the road, the headlights illuminated the evergreens, alders, and hemlock trees that blanketed both sides of them.

"Where does this lead?"

Cam slowed as the road got a little rougher. "There's an area to park just a little farther. I don't think anyone will come looking for us here."

They eventually pulled off the road, to a makeshift lot of dirt and gravel, probably scraped by a park-service bulldozer but otherwise empty. Cam turned off the car, and the silence of the immensely dark forest enveloped them.

"Are you hungry?" Cam said.

"No, not really."

As her eyes began to adjust in the darkness, Val heard the rustling of the grocery bag.

"I picked up some Bactine," Cam said, and Val felt her fingers as they reached out to her.

She got out her cell phone and clicked on the light app, holding it while Cam dabbed at her cuts. She resisted the urge to jump each time Cam found a new injury, and when she was done, Val said, "I just can't figure out what Donna, Nedra, and Mack have in common. What the hell do they want?"

"Whatever it is, they want it enough to hurt you in order to get it."

Val took the Bactine from Cam. "Gimme," she said, and Cam put her arms out. She dabbed Cam's cuts and scrapes, taking a moment to enjoy the feel of her arms. They were firm yet soft. Val hated that they were now crisscrossed with branch trails.

She finished and put the first-aid bottle back in the bag. When she sat back, Cam put her arm around her, and she leaned in to her. She couldn't remember the last time she felt comforted.

She looked out into the darkness and her mind began to wander. She imagined flying in an airplane, ten or twenty thousand feet above them. Sometimes that worked when she was at her job and needed to back up and look at the big picture. She saw her mom's house and Mack's garage. She traveled north to the place on the road where she'd had the accident. She thought about where she'd been coming from. She flew over the Portland airport and the hospital where she'd picked up her mother's car. She sailed through the clouds and finally came to rest in her mom's front yard. The for-sale sign was there.

"Cam?"

"Hmm?"

"I just can't picture my mom hanging out with Nedra Tobias. They're total opposites. Maybe the whole church connection serves as some kind of grand equalizer, I don't know. Mom didn't seem to have a lot of friends, so maybe the few from the church and the theater were good enough for her, but Nedra?"

"I know. She's like the Ursula of the Oregon Coast."

Val laughed and Cam joined in.

When they settled back down, Cam said quietly, "What did your mom die of?"

"Sudden arrhythmic death. I read about it online. It said something about the fact that in one in twenty cases, there's no definitive cause of death. It just happens. Even an expert cardiac doctor sometimes can't determine why."

Val inhaled deeply. Even though she hadn't been in touch that much, she really missed her mom. "I guess we'll never know. You can't autopsy ashes."

Cam hugged her tighter.

Val paused, going over their close call at Mack's garage. "We could be in deep shit, you know."

"I know."

"I'm a bit freaked out," Val said. "I can't go to jail."

"We won't. We'll figure something out."

They fell silent, and Val went over and over every detail of her last few days. Everything seemed connected, but then again, nothing did. The gas incident at her house might not have been tied to the beating she got. Nedra could simply be a realtor and no more. Mack, however, was a sick fuck, that she knew for sure, but that fact didn't seem to be related to anything else. Sure, he knew the girl from the accident, but pretty much everybody knew everybody in Hemlock.

"My head is spinning from all this," she said, stifling a yawn.

Cam reached over Val's lap, grabbing the grocery bag, and pulled out the blanket she'd bought. She unfolded it and gently placed it over them.

"I'm not that tired."

"Just try to sleep for a while. We've got a long day ahead of us."

Val slouched down in her seat, more exhausted than she'd realized. Cam turned the ignition key to auxiliary and powered the stereo on. The voice of a religious man in the middle of a rather fervent sermon rose and fell as if he was galloping toward judgment day. Thunderous words like wrath and serpent made the speakers on the dash hum as he warned his listeners to shun the devil's invitation to temptation's party. Cam changed stations, trolling across the airwaves, until she found some soft rock.

"Just some music for a little while to chill out to. We won't wear the battery down."

A silence settled between them as they listened to a James Taylor song.

"Mr. Harlin's a nice man," Val eventually said.

"He is. He's lived a long, interesting life, and he's as true blue as they come. It's like the modern world hasn't influenced him at all. He has no cell phone or Internet. He reads the paper and listens to his radio or watches old movies on TV."

"He called you the real McCoy and even said applesauce!" Val laughed. "He said he hadn't driven his car much since twenty aught nine. Other than my mom, I don't know many people who say *aught*."

"It's refreshing that he's such a simple guy. When I'm at his house, I can relax and not worry about anything. It's like you go back in time there, you know?"

Cam inhaled deeply, and Val suddenly sat farther upright.

"Val?"

"Aught," she said as if Cam understood, which she couldn't have. She pulled out the paper. "Look. One, aught, as in one, zero. These are dates!"

"Let me see," Cam said, and Val shared the paper.

"Look at this first listing. One, zero. That's October. Zero, five. That's the day. October fifth."

"Nine, three…'93? No, wait a second. Nine, three, zero. That's not the year." Cam looked up at Val. "It's the time."

"Is that when the house was first listed, maybe?"

"Why would that be important, especially the exact time?"

"True."

"Even if they were times, these would all be dates and times that occurred after your mom wrote the list." She pointed to the date written in the top corner.

"She wrote October fourth. You're right. All of these numbers, or dates, occur after that time."

Cam scanned the paper. "And, as of today, all of these dates have passed…except for one."

Val read aloud the numbers next to the address for the church. "One, zero, one, four, one zero, three, zero."

"October fourteenth. That's tomorrow night. At ten thirty."

"Something's going to happen tomorrow. Should we go to the police?"

Cam scrunched her eyebrows together. "I don't think so. I doubt they'd believe an ounce of what we said. They wouldn't think this paper was tied to anything. Even if they were interested in playing ball, they'd say they'd have to do their own investigation. And based on what evidence we don't have, on something we don't even understand, tomorrow will have come and gone before they'd act on it."

An Elton John song was now playing on the radio, and they both fell into silence again.

Cam moved her arm up onto the back of Val's seat and gently pulled Val toward her. Leaning against Cam's shoulder, she gave in to the offer of safety and comfort, something she not only wanted but also needed.

With her head on Cam's shoulder, she listened to her breathing. The cadence was as calming as a hypnotic watch, swinging from a chain. In this moment, the world grew tranquil and time stopped, allowing her to just...be.

Sometime later, Cam turned off the radio and the sounds of the forest took over again. From just outside the car, the rustling of trees almost sounded like rain. The car's engine still ticked every so often as it cooled down, and the staccato trilling of what might have been a Western screech owl came from somewhere not too far away.

Cam adjusted her butt in the seat, and Val felt her wince.

"One of your cuts?"

"One I didn't know about."

Val reached for her cell phone and clicked the light back on. She took the Bactine from the bag at her feet as Cam inspected her left arm.

Close to the crook of her elbow, Val found the cut and applied the antiseptic. She then felt around, making sure there were no more scrapes, running her fingers along the muscles in Cam's forearm, brushing across it with light touches.

Cam laid her head back and murmured, "That feels nice."

Val turned off her phone and dropped it and the antiseptic on the floorboard, wondering if she should stop. Given that she was still unsure of practically everything that had transpired since she'd arrived in Hemlock, she probably should, but the human contact felt wonderful. She could feel Cam relaxing, but touching Cam was just as soothing to her. She needed a break, a chance to catch her breath and calm down. And despite her uncertainty about Cam, her attraction was growing.

As Val massaged her arm, Cam reached over and steadied her hand on Val's leg. Then she began rubbing Val's thigh, and a mixture of relaxation and arousal washed over her. She closed her eyes, allowing only the feeling of each other's fingers to fill her mind. And slowly, as their hands began traveling in widening circles, Val's heartbeat accelerated and she tightened her thighs, not to stop the sensations she was feeling, but to heighten the throbbing between them.

Cam must have been feeling the same way, because she moaned slightly when she exhaled.

In the darkness, Val let her head spin from the disorientation but, more powerfully, from the heady arousal taking over every part of her increasingly stimulated body.

She marveled at the pleasure that saturated her like an invigorating spring shower, washing over her body with velvet fluidity. Simply from Cam's hand brushing across her pants, squeezing periodically, Val's breathing quickened as if she were being drawn under a sensual, but escalating, spell.

Cam moaned again, so quietly that it screamed in Val's ears, its fervent declaration sounding sexy but controlled, as if Cam was trying to keep her own desire a secret or, even sexier, was unable to restrain her response to the sensation.

Val ached, needing more. She was losing control and allowed her hand to drop to Cam's leg, mirroring the strokes she was receiving on her own thigh. Ever so slightly, Cam writhed in her seat, holding her breath and then fighting its escape, as if she was struggling to contain all of her normal bodily functions.

Not a word had passed between them for a long while, but the air was teeming with the intense unspoken exchanges.

Cam seemed to be fighting her desire, which only stoked the flames erupting in Val's stomach and between her legs. Just picturing what Cam might feel like or how incredibly amazing she would taste destroyed whatever restraint she had left. Val's mouth found Cam's neck and she kissed her, slowly licking and circling her lips over the delicate skin she found there.

She felt Cam squeeze her thigh, harder now, and Val moved her hand higher up Cam's leg. Cam responded by raising her hips with such yielding subtlety that Val almost passed out.

She reached up and turned Cam's face toward her, again finding her mouth not only open, but also searching for hers. They kissed as if the act would soon be outlawed, reluctant to stop and driven to make up for every second they'd spent not kissing.

Val wanted Cam with the ferocity of a thousand volcanoes, surprised at the scorching heat she felt. It was like uncontrollable molten rock that must have always been inside her, but had lain dormant until now. Its potential eruption and consequent devastation scared her and propelled her at the same time. She was incapable and unwilling to stop now.

Cam's muffled moans matched hers as Val dropped her hand, finding the spot between Cam's legs that caused Cam to raise her hips even higher. She felt Cam's thighs part, consenting to whatever Val wanted. The heat that radiated there was intense, and all Val wanted to do was climb inside her.

As she massaged the tightness she felt, Cam kissed her harder. Their breathing became so loud, the symphony of muffled exhales mounting, that all sounds coming from the forest disappeared.

Cam pushed away suddenly and, in one swift motion, backed through the space between the front seats and pulled Val with her. They landed in the backseat, and when Cam flipped her onto her back, Val grabbed Cam's shirt, tugging it off her. Their mouths found each other again as Cam lowered herself onto Val, straddling her hips on the challengingly narrow backseat.

The bra had to go as well, and it unsnapped with the first flick of Val's hand. Cam raised herself up, twisting her shoulders until it dropped off her. In the dark, Val could barely see her breasts, but she rose to meet them with her mouth. Cam balanced herself by holding onto the back of the front seat as Val alternated kissing and lightly sucking each breast.

Murmurs of arousal came from Cam, and Val took that moment to unsnap Cam's pants. She tugged the zipper down and glided her hand inside, slipping beneath Cam's underwear, and immediately found the searing wetness she craved.

Cam cried out, arching her head back, and Val stopped kissing her breasts to listen more than watch from her perfect position underneath. When Cam began to rock against her hand, Val slipped two fingers inside her. With her other hand, Val held on to Cam's hip, steadying her and holding her captive at the same time.

Around her swirling fingers, Val felt her shudder and groan. Cam then lowered her upper body until they were nose to nose. She could now see Cam's eyes and the concentrated intensity that had overtaken them. Cam didn't need to say anything; the look begged her not to stop. And she didn't.

They were now panting in unison, and Val became so turned on, she thrust deeper. Cam gasped and kissed her as they moved together.

Val's own clit was throbbing, and she was sure that if they kept this up, she'd come without being touched. When she withdrew her hand slightly to rub Cam's clit, Cam began rocking from side to side and sucked on Val's tongue as they kissed.

Cam's breathing quickened, and the shudders came again. Val sensed she'd found Cam's sweet spot so she kept up the rhythm, moaning encouragement as she spurred her on. Cam began trembling and broke their kiss, lifting herself up just a few inches from Val's face. She squeezed her eyes tightly together for a few seconds, and when she opened them, Val saw the most intoxicated gaze she'd ever witnessed.

Cam's eyebrows rose in surrender and her lips parted slightly. Her arms and hips began to shake and her expression deepened, drawing Val in with her. Cam's breathing quieted momentarily, and then she suddenly cried out loudly as her orgasm pounded against Val's fingers. As each wave gripped her, Cam stared into Val's eyes. And Val saw the sacred center of her desire.

Val was completely mesmerized by the sight, succumbing to Cam's needs and so devoted to this pleasure she didn't intend to stop until Cam made her.

And when she did, Cam made love to her, slowly at first and then with a passion so fiery, Val knew for the first time what being thoroughly consumed felt like.

Though the car was parked among the trees of Cascade Head, Val was now speeding down a nameless road, with Cam's arms tight around her and well aware that she wore no safety belt.

Chapter Fifteen

Val awoke with Cam's arms wrapped around her and a slight cramp in her side. They'd fallen asleep sometime in the middle of the night and stayed in their spooned position, but she wasn't sure how the blanket had ended up pulled over them. When she moved to relieve the cramp, Cam began to stir.

Val sat up, bringing part of the blanket with her, and squinted into the morning sun that was peering through the trees.

Two other cars were parked in the trailhead lot, one devoid of people, and on the bumper of the other sat a man who was tying his running shoes. He finished, checked his watch, and then took off running up the trail.

She wrapped the blanket tighter to fend off the chill of the Oregon morning and listened to the birds as they chirped and rustled cheerfully in the forest around them. She massaged her face, trying to drive the drowsiness away. Taking stock of her surroundings, she saw remnants of the night before littering the car. Anyone peeking in would think, with all the clothes draped over seats and wrinkled on the floorboards, that they were homeless.

Cam sat up and Val turned to kiss her.

"Good morning."

"Good morning." Cam rubbed her eyes. "What time is it?"

"Almost seven."

Cam stretched and yawned while Val ran a hand through her disheveled hair.

"You look beautiful," Cam said.

Val eyed her sideways. "I bet you say that to all your backseat girls."

Cam laughed. "I do. Seeing as you're the only one I've ever had."

Val was still attempting to tame her hair when Cam caught her hand in hers. She pulled it toward her and kissed her fingers, one at a time.

"Are you okay?"

Val's first response was a resounding yes. Her body felt the exertions from the night before and her muscles were tired and sore, but it was a satisfied discomfort. Her bones and skin were happily invigorated and completely content.

Her mind, however, needed to catch up with the events of the night before. She should question the rationality of her decisions and weigh the possibility that she'd just stepped into a dangerous situation. A part of her still wondered why Cam had been aloof and questioned her true connection to Donna, Nedra, Mack, and the others.

But right now, Cam sat next to her and the blanket failed to cover one of her beautiful breasts. The scratchy wool fabric against her soft skin was one of the sexiest juxtapositions Val had ever taken in. With Cam's body so close and her sleepy eyes looking so damn sexy, Val had no desire to pay attention to her rational self.

"I'm very okay," Val said. "How about you?"

"I'm a little surprised but very happy." Cam's smile was delicate, as if she'd just grown shy. "And I really like you."

"I'm pretty into you, too."

They found their clothing and made a fairly good attempt to avoid the awkwardness of dressing in the backseat of a car. Cam finished and climbed into the front seat, retrieving the grocery bag and rummaging through it.

After Val finished dressing and tying her shoes, she opened the backseat door. She stepped out into the crisp morning and stretched, reaching as far up to the treetops as she could. It was a spectacular morning. The fog was burning off, and the pine trees presented their perfumed needles to the wind to help freshen the day.

Cam rolled down the driver's window and offered Val a bottle of water.

Val took a long draw. "What about Donna?

"What about Donna?"

"From what I remember, she loved cars."

"She did?"

"Yeah. And beaches. And strangers' porches, behind the candy counter at the Bijou—"

"Donna Laufstrom?" Cam sounded truly astonished.

"Yes. But that was a long time ago. I suppose she was just being a crazy kid."

"Well, she wasn't that way by the time I met her. She was more shy and reserved."

"Donna Laufstrom?"

That made Cam grin.

"Seems like she ended up being two different people," Val said, handing the water back to Cam.

"Three, actually."

"You mean the way she also changed right before you split up?"

"Yeah."

"Sounds like she reverted back to her crazy self. Like the way she was in high school."

"It was as if one day she just decided to change," Cam said. "Did she ever wear leather pants and jackets back then?"

Val shook her head.

Cam grew silent, her head nodding slightly as if she was making a decision. She began to tell a story that must have been roaming around in her head, confused and itinerant, for quite a long time. "Toward the end with us, things got strange. She hid sex toys in the closet—toys she never showed me. She started computer searches on sex and porn websites, but only when I was at work.

"I didn't say anything about it. I was in shock, I guess. I thought maybe it was some strange phase. Stupid me. I thought it'd pass. Then one day when I was in the laundry room, I picked up an extra box of laundry detergent, thinking it was empty. As I threw it in the trash, I could tell something was in the box. It was photographs. Porn.

"Except not of women. Or even men. They were of really young guys. Junior-high-school boys or something like that. Pretty heavy bondage stuff. Jesus, the kids looked thirteen."

Cam stared down at her hands. "I'm not sure what caused the change. It was like she was questioning her sexual feelings. I guess she began to search for the answer somewhere else. Looking back to when we met, she was quite nervous about sex. Maybe timid is more the word. But then I think about what she got into after that…all that kinky stuff. How could she feel comfortable with that? I don't understand it. I don't know what happened."

"She was pretty religious when we were in school. Not that it affected her then, but maybe it did later."

"She did go to church all the time," Cam said. "She'd already started something with Mack when we were still together, and he had something to do with it."

Val looked out the window. She began to say something but stopped. The early morning woods looked beautiful. A few bright streaks of sunshine lit up leaves that glowed bright green as the rays cut through the trees.

"It makes sense. Mack's recording unsuspecting women in the bathroom for his own jollies." Val rested her hands against the driver's doorframe. "Mack knows we're onto him. But do you think he knows about me on the video camera?"

"I don't know. I sure wish I had my hands on the tape."

"Well, you said the video recorder's got to be in his office. All we have to do is pop the tape out and run."

"If it's there."

Val wondered what the chances were. "It's worth a try to see."

"How do you propose we do that? We can't disarm the alarm without knowing the code."

"We go when the alarm's not on. During daytime hours."

"So after he tried to kill us last night," Cam said, "we just waltz in there and get the tape?"

"What's he going to do? Shoot you in front of all his customers?"

"Oh, I guess I just got volunteered." Cam smiled warmly and reached out, and Val took her hand. "So I walk into his garage and right into his office and grab the videotape?"

"No, *I* walk into the garage and *you* grab the videotape."

"And what are you doing while I'm grabbing the tape?"

"Creating a diversion."

"I was afraid you were going to say that."

"What? It's a great idea."

Cam hesitated, glancing at Val with a crooked grin that looked full of trepidation.

"Then we go to the police. Okay?"

Val leaned over and kissed her. "Okay."

"I can't believe we're even talking about this."

"I can't believe we spent the night in Mr. Harlin's car in the middle of the forest." Val stroked her cheek.

A faint warning bell rang in the recesses of her brain, alerting her that she'd crossed a line that couldn't be reversed. But she'd known when she'd first massaged Cam's arm the night before that she was taking a step into the dark void of uncertainty. However, she was so tired and touching Cam felt so good that she allowed her body to wrench control from her hesitant brain. And while she might come to regret her decision, her body was thanking her for feeling so refreshed and satisfied.

Cam and Val sat on Mr. Harlin's couch while he rested in his easy chair. Jesus and the Virgin Mary still stood sentry over the room. In the background, a sermon on the evils of premarital sex emanated from the television.

"Necco wafer?"

Val thanked him as she took the Apostles jar. She took a few and handed it to Cam.

"Thank you for lending us your car." Cam tipped the jar as well and then gave it back to him. "Would it be possible to keep it for another day or so?"

Mr. Harlin studied them and gestured to Val. "Best I can figure, you've got a husband, and that's why you two are here."

Val almost laughed, but she didn't think the Virgin Marys would find the same comment amusing. "No, sir!"

"We just need to keep a low profile," Cam said. "And we hope we can spend the day here. We'd rather not be out and about."

Mr. Harlin crunched on a Necco wafer. "Hell, I don't need to know what's going on. Most of the time, I don't want anyone to know my business either. And a lot of folk around here have busy noses." He made a sniffing sound, and this time Val laughed.

"Damn dogs," he said.

Cam stood up. "Can I get you anything?"

"There's coffee on the stove. Might need to be heated up a bit. Do you mind?"

"Of course not." Cam left the room saying, "I'll pour us three cups."

"Cam, there, is a good kid," Mr. Harlin said when they heard a cabinet door open in the kitchen. "Always keeps me in candy. Ran some errands for me when I hurt my back." He shifted in his chair and looked like he was struggling in pain. "Don't believe the town folk about her." He settled down. "No one gossips about other people's virtues." He shook a finger in the air. "Bertrand Russell said that."

"Three coffees, here." Cam came out of the kitchen and handed each one a mug.

"Where are you from, Val?"

"Dallas. But I used to live here."

"What's your last name?"

"Montague."

"Kris's child?"

"Yes. Did you know her?"

"Not well, but I had a few scrapes with one of her boyfriends a long time ago."

"Which one?"

"Dan something or other. What a dewdropper."

"Well, he didn't last long. He drank. A lot."

"That's what the fight was over. Seems he didn't like the way I pumped his gas. Too damn slow, he said. That was back when I owned a 76 station south of town. I told him I didn't like him driving all lit up like he was. Your mom was in the car and she looked scared. Of him or his driving, I'm not sure. Faster than I knew it, he snapped his cap and got out of the car. Took a swing at me. Being as hooched up as he was, he was like one of those weeble-wobble toys, so I ducked and came back with a fist of my own. Split his nose pretty good, and by the time he got to pinching back all that blood and screaming and cursing me, I had a crowbar from the garage in my hand. I used it to point out the direction he needed to leave."

"Wow."

"Funny thing was," Mr. Harlin said as he popped another Necco in his mouth, "your mom looked at me as they pulled out of the station and mouthed 'thank you.' Never forgot that."

"You never told me that story, Mr. Harlin."

"Well, Cam, if I told you every story I have, those chocolates of yours would never get made, now would they?"

"I guess not."

"Now, you know I'm not dumb." Mr. Harlin adjusted in his chair again. "So I figure you all are in some kind of trouble. You don't need to tell me anything. I'm just happy for the company."

"It's not trouble we ever asked for."

Mr. Harlin seemed to recognize the difference as easily as one could identify black from white. "I understand."

"Well, Mr. Harlin, we have one thing we have to do today, but otherwise, we'll hang out with you, okay?"

"That'd be a hell of a nice thing for you to do."

Val walked into Mack's waiting room first. Luckily, three women and a man were sitting there. Two children played by the front counter, but Val had no idea whose they were. The man politely stood to offer Val his seat, but she waved him off.

"I won't be here long, but thank you."

Mack walked in from the garage, wiping his hands on a greasy rag. The moment he looked up, his eyes narrowed.

Before he could say anything, Val started in on him. "I want to know what's going on with my car. I've been waiting for days and days, and no one has called me. I just looked in your garage, and it looks more banged up than when I brought it in. What kind of business are you running here?" She ran her sentences together, partly because she didn't want to give him a chance to respond but also because she was more nervous than a tin man in a lightning storm.

"You must think you can take advantage of an out-of-towner. Or maybe it's because I'm a woman. But just look at my car!" She turned to the man who'd offered her his seat. "You won't believe the damage it's received since it arrived here." She began to walk out the door Mack had come through. "What have you done to it? Are you doing the same to these poor people as well?" By now the customers looked pretty surprised, but Mack's face hadn't changed. It was flushed red with contempt.

She walked into the garage, hoping he'd follow her. She gestured to the male customer. "Which car is yours? Have you checked it to make sure he's not scamming you, too?" She stepped through the door, raising her voice as she did. "You better stop working on my car! I'm going to call my insurance agent. He's going to want to hear about this fraudulent business you're running here!"

When she was six or seven feet inside, she turned around and almost smacked into Mack's face. He was seething, his nostrils puffed out like a dragon's did right before releasing a firestorm.

"What are you going to do about it?!" She yelled as loud as she could, which was easy to do because his rapid appearance had scared the hell out of her.

Mack's voice rolled out as a slow growl, low and menacing. "What the fuck do you think you're doing?"

"I'm here to find out what you're doing with my car!"

Glancing over Mack's shoulder, Val could see through the window of the waiting room door that the customers had gathered around, watching them like they'd just arrived at a Las Vegas prizefight. Behind them, Val saw Cam dart by, toward Mack's office.

"Look, you fucked-up little bitch. I know what you and Cam did."

Val was well within punching distance, and every ounce of her screamed to back away from Mack's face, but she didn't dare lose her momentum. "Now you wait a minute! I brought my car in and trusted you. I needed help and I thought you'd be an honest mechanic!" She had to keep the charade up as long as she could, so when he tried to speak again, she rambled on. "I'm a single mother! I have three children to raise all by myself! And you want to drain my bank account to fix the car that they need to go to school in! How incorrigible is that?"

His eyes burned through hers and he snarled back. "The police are looking for you right now. I suggest you get the hell out of here before I pound your face in."

"Ten more days? You're going to keep it ten more days?"

Cam darted behind the customers and out the front door.

"That's it," he said. "I'm calling the police."

That was her cue to leave. She walked around him and back through the waiting-room door. The customers moved out of the way, and she headed quickly for the front door.

"Is an honest mechanic too much to ask for?" she said, exited the waiting room, and double-timed it to the side street where Cam was waiting.

Cam had the car started when Val jumped in.

"Oh, we really need to get the heck out of here."

Cam drove across Coast Highway and took back streets to avoid the squad cars they knew would be heading toward Mack's.

"Did you get it?" Val said, her pulse still racing.

She held up two tapes. "I found the recorder on top of a credenza that shares the wall with the bathroom, but it was empty, so I searched around his desk. I found a stack of tapes in a cabinet, behind some cleaning materials. I took the two that were on top of the pile. They both say, 'Edited tape.' I'm not sure if one of these is the one with you on it, but I didn't have much time."

Val took one from her, staring at the very old cassette. "It's…a VHS tape."

"It was the only recorder in his office. It makes sense, though. Any recording device you'd buy today usually sends files to a server, even a Cloud server. Given the lady porn he's been getting, I don't think Mack wanted that. He must be converting and editing the tapes on his own."

"Shit," Val said, waving the little black fossil. "How the heck are we going to see what's on this?"

Cam smiled at her mischievously." You forget who's harboring us."

❖

"Of course I got a VHS machine," Mr. Harlin said as he let them in the door. Cam turned to Val and smiled again. He waved them in and noticed that they were carrying the metal plate and big spring but only glanced at them.

As Mr. Harlin sat in his easy chair and Val sat on the couch, Cam knelt down and loaded one of the tapes in a dusty machine that sat under the television. A number of other cassette tapes were piled on either side, and Cam could tell they were mostly old Western movies and documentaries on the Vietnam War.

"I need to warn you, Mr. Harlin," Cam said as she stood up and backed over to the couch, "we think Mack's been secretly filming women who go in to use his bathroom at the garage. I'm not sure exactly who's on this one, but we felt it was important to stop him from doing this."

"Okay," he said slowly.

Cam pointed the remote toward the television and looked at Val with a nervous but hopeful smile. She seemed to be saying, "We're in this together and it's going to be okay." But then again, maybe that's what Val wanted to see in Cam's expression because she so desperately needed the reassurance.

Cam clicked the remote and the television hissed from the white noise on the screen. A few seconds later, the screen went black.

"Uh-oh," Cam said.

"Let's wait a bit. Remember, the camera's somehow rigged to the light switch and doesn't start until someone turns the light on."

They waited only a few more seconds and the image went from black to stark white, and then, as the lens auto-focused, they were looking down, through a square grid pattern to the toilet below.

Cam pointed, saying to Mr. Harlin, "That's the grill the camera's hiding behind."

A child came into view. The little girl struggled with her pants and then climbed onto the toilet. In the inappropriateness that was playing out before them, they all looked away.

The tape went black again as the little girl turned off the light and left. There was an obvious edit on the tape, and then a few seconds later, the light came back on and another little girl walked in. This happened several more times. At once, Val and Cam looked at each other.

Cam's eyes widened. "He's not taping women…"

Mr. Harlin smacked his hand on the side table next to him. "That goddamn bastard is filming children."

"Holy shit," Val said, then quickly glanced up at the largest of the Virgin Mary pictures, silently apologizing.

"That's just sick." Cam turned the VHS player off.

Val watched her face drop. Cam looked down at the carpet, and Val wondered if she was thinking about how it would affect Donna.

"If I were a few years younger," Mr. Harlin said, "I'd go over there and put that man in the ground."

"Val," Cam said suddenly. "We've got these tapes to nail that pervert Mack, but I think it's time we told Mr. Harlin what's been happening to you."

CHAPTER SIXTEEN

It took an hour to lay out for Mr. Harlin the series of events since Val arrived in town. They showed him the metal plate and the spring, and he examined both of them, turning them over in his hands.

He listened, mostly, and when they had finally explained the need to stay at his house that day, he said, "You've stepped into a big pile of manure, haven't you?"

"Yes," Val replied.

"Mack's not a person you want to mess with, I can tell you that, but I don't see you have much choice in the matter. And the story does sound a little soft around the edges." He leaned forward in his chair, lifting the metal plate and bouncing it up and down a little. "It might be a bit farfetched for the police to believe the catapult idea, but if anyone's gonna come up with that contraption, it'd be Mack. He's a mechanic and a hunter. He's not smart enough to plan the exact time you'd be driving along the highway, though. And I doubt he could have come up with the gas-burner-on-the-stove trick." He tapped the side of his head. "His elevator doesn't go all the way up to the top floor."

"I believe that's where Nedra comes in."

Mr. Harlin leaned back. "She's the Marie Antoinette of Hemlock, all right. That woman thinks she owns this town. And maybe she does. She's been known to bully people for what she wants. There've been more than a few houses and businesses the owners were forced to sell."

"We just can't figure out what they're after," Val said.

"If it ain't about love, then follow the money."

"The only clue we have is that church's address on the list," Cam said as she checked her watch.

"You wanna take my gun?" Mr. Harlin said. "I've got a .40 caliber heater you can borrow."

"No," Cam said. "That would get us into even more trouble."

"Then send Mack over here and I'll take care of that pervert."

Cam chuckled. "I wouldn't cry at his funeral." She turned to Val. "We've got a few hours until we have to go to the church."

Val nodded, but her stomach coiled up in apprehension. She had no idea what they'd discover, if anything. And as nervous as she was, they needed something more to take to the police. If they came up with nothing, they could find themselves behind bars with no ability to help themselves or solve the mystery.

Either way, the thought of going to the church that night chilled her to the bone.

❖

Val was more stressed out than she could remember. She shook inside like she'd just been dropped into a ten-foot snowdrift in the middle of a Siberian winter. She tried to sit still in Mr. Harlin's car, but her legs kept jerking. She wasn't sure what they'd find at the church, but just being out on the streets, knowing that at any moment the police could pull them over, made her paranoid. Just get us to the church, she chanted silently.

Cam took side streets since most of them were void of streetlights. Val remembered playing as a child with some of the other neighborhood kids. They'd make up games or fight scenarios and play them out for hours on end, staying outside as late as they could. When the sun began to set, they strained to see where they were going or where their imagined enemies were lurking during their impromptu street games.

Now she was traveling down some of these same streets, as an adult on a much different adventure, and hoping no real enemies were actually lurking about.

Cam stopped shy of every street corner, pausing to see if any squad cars were roaming around. They saw very few cars at all, since it was after ten o'clock at night. With most of the stores shut down in Hemlock, virtually no one ventured out this late. In house after house that they passed, lights were on, and bluish images from televisions moved and shifted on the drapes in the front rooms.

About three blocks from the church, they glanced at each other and Cam reached over to hold Val's hand. She slowed to a stop on the corner and looked down the cross street, but they were the only ones on the road.

"The tapes we have might not be the one that had you on it," Cam said. "Maybe Mack didn't tell the police about us because he wants to come after us himself. But then again, if he has the right one, he could still give it to the police."

"I suppose I'll deal with that if and when it happens." Val was certainly afraid of being arrested for breaking and entering the garage, but she was too sickened by Mack to care much. "He'd have to edit the tape to show only me in the bathroom, which I think would make the police question why. He's absolutely not going to show them those children. And if he only showed a clip of me, how could he prove it was after hours?"

"You're right. The tapes aren't time-stamped."

"That's because he never intended to use them for security reasons."

Cam leaned over and kissed her. In the dark of the same car, the night before came rushing back to Val, making her remember every spot where Cam had touched her. She thought of Cam straddling her and her own hand sliding down Cam's pants, and the image made her suddenly light-headed.

She looked at Cam, who was now concentrating on rolling through the intersection. Why shouldn't Val believe her wholeheartedly? She'd been with her every step of the way, and they were side by side when they broke into Mack's place. But then again, if she were still tight with Donna, Mack wouldn't implicate Cam. She just needed one thing she could believe was entirely true, one fact she could put her complete trust in and then puzzle out the rest of the details. She'd arrived in town utterly unprepared for the strange events that had unfolded so rapidly. And Cam had come into her life right when she needed her and so perfectly that when Val realized Cam had shared a bed and a life with Donna, the luck she'd come upon suddenly seemed a little too perfect.

Things had transpired so quickly that trying to pin down just one reliable, solid truth was like grabbing a matchstick in the middle of a tornado. It was probably appropriate that they were on their way to a church because Val now prayed she'd survive whatever swiftly approaching twister was coming her way.

CHAPTER SEVENTEEN

Cam drove past The Seeds of Light church and turned at the next corner to park. She killed the engine and the dashboard lights went dark. From where they sat they could see the front parking lot of the church. And though the lot had a couple of streetlamps shining cones of light downward, the church sat in shadow, its windows malevolent, black eyes staring back at them.

Val strained to see any movement around the building or in the parking lot. “It doesn’t look like anyone’s there.”

Cam checked her watch. “It’s a quarter past ten. If this is what your mom’s note was referring to, we have a few minutes.”

“I assume there’s an entrance in the back. We might not see anyone if they arrive that way.”

“Unless they drive off-road, through the trees back there, they still have to drive past here.” Cam pointed to a driveway on the side of the church. “That’s the only way to the back.”

How would she know that, Val wondered. She hadn’t said that she’d ever come to this church. But then again, she probably knew almost every road and parking lot in this small town. The anticipation that stuck like a too-big piece of taffy candy in her throat was making her panic and doubt everything. She felt like she was about to find out everything she needed to know but wasn’t sure it would fix what had been going so wrong.

They sat in silence and Val stared at the church, looking for someone inside to open a door or walk past a window. She was really spooked, and her gut was churning as if some completely oblivious farmer was using her stomach to make five pounds of butter.

She turned ever so slightly to look at Cam, who was engrossed in studying the church and surrounding parking lot. Val scrutinized her face, trying to read her. What was behind Cam's reticence at their first kiss, and why had she seemed to pull back? Why was Cam so available to her when she had a business to run? And why, when Cam had spent all her life with these people, even loving one of them, would she side with Val and help her so unreservedly?

Cam's face brightened suddenly, and Val realized that a car had just turned a corner close by and its headlights were shining on her.

"Look," Cam said.

An El Camino pulled into the church's front parking lot and parked in a space close to the front door. There were, maybe, three people inside, but it was hard to tell. The headlights and brake lights shut off, but no one got out.

"Who's that, can you tell?"

"Nobody I know."

Presently, another car approached. A pickup truck pulled in and parked next to the El Camino. The lights went out, but whoever was in it remained where they were, too.

"That's Mack's truck. That's got to be Donna with him."

Val saw another car approach, and the churning in her stomach accelerated. "Shit," she said as a Tesla pulled in.

"Nedra Tobias."

When Nedra parked, the doors of all three vehicles opened.

Three people got out of the El Camino. Val squinted, straining to see who they were, and it took less than a second for her eyes to lock onto the shortest one.

"That's the girl! The girl from the accident!"

"I don't know who she is. I've never seen her before," Cam said, then pointed quickly. "Shit. You're seeing what I'm seeing, aren't you?"

The other two were the men that had helped Mack the night they'd chased Val and Cam into the woods. Val definitely recognized the Dingo boots and enjoyed a nanosecond of satisfaction when she saw the man's heavily bandaged chin. They stepped around the car to stand with the girl by the trunk. Mack and Donna had already gotten out of the truck and joined them. The Tesla driver's door opened and Nedra stepped out. Too afraid and too engrossed to look away, Val stared at the activity as if her very life depended on her retention of every detail.

Val watched Nedra walk over to the passenger side of her car and open the door. Val leaned forward, so engrossed she could no longer see anything beyond the periphery of her tunnel vision. Her throat had gone desert dry and she barely got the words out. "Who's getting out of her car?"

"It looks like a little boy."

The group of seven walked into the church, and one by one, lights began to come on behind the window drapery. The church no longer looked foreboding, but Val's senses were on fire with the knowledge that malevolence lived within some of the people now inside it.

She tapped the dashboard, her fingers attempting to release some of the energy that was fighting containment in what felt like a pressure cooker in her body.

"What the hell are they gathering for?"

"Whatever it is, your mom knew about it and felt it was important enough to write down." Cam took the keys out of the ignition. "Let's go find out."

Cam and Val silently made their way over to the church. They stayed close to the building, ducking under windows, and headed around to the back. Sneaking up to a back door, they listened for sounds. Val glanced at Cam and shook her head. She didn't hear anything.

Slowly, Cam tried the knob. It was locked.

Val motioned for her to follow and she crept to a window. Its drapes were closed, but a muffled voice speaking intermittently softly and loudly was coming from what Val guessed was the church's sanctuary. She jiggled the frame but it was locked, too. She proceeded down the back of the building, trying windows, but they were all shut tight.

Finally, she came upon one window, and though it was locked, the drapes were parted a few inches. The people from the parking lot were sitting in the first-row pew, and Pastor Kind stood behind a pulpit that sat on a raised platform.

"He had to have already been here, waiting for them," Val said.

The pastor's voice was much clearer, and he was strangely animated as he spoke, looking like a mentally ill person rocking to the voices in his head.

"The rapture of which I speak," Pastor Kind said, "comes in a special form. It takes the very sensitive parishioners to see that. You see, theology and sex are sometimes confused in the…" he gestured dramatically with his hands "…the gray convergence of that rapture."

Cam whispered to Val, "What is this? A private worship group?"

"They're closer than you might think." Pastor Kind rocked back and forth. "How exposed do you feel when you're worshipping the deities? And how exposed do you feel when you're worshipping the flesh?" He raised his fist. "Does it feel the same?"

The group leaned forward in their seats, seemingly transfixed by his words.

"And why does it feel the same?" Pastor Kind slammed his fist down on the pulpit. "Because it IS the same!"

He paused and then said, "Nedra, please come up here. And Manny, bring the child."

Nedra walked up to the pulpit, and Dingo Boots took the boy by the hand and walked him up there, too. The child appeared indifferent about what was going on.

Pastor Kind stepped from the pulpit and took the child by the hand, and Dingo Boots backed away. The pastor then handed the boy off to Nedra.

Pastor Kind returned to the pulpit and gestured to Nedra. "Hug the child."

Nedra obeyed, hugging the child, who flinched a little. Val wondered if the boy knew her at all. Certainly, if his family were members of the church, the little boy would be familiar with who she was.

Pastor Kind said, "How did that feel?"

Val was surprised when the group answered with "great" and "wonderful."

"What the hell is this?" Val said to Cam.

But before Cam could answer, Nedra grabbed the child by his arms and threw him at the pulpit. A terrible scream erupted from the boy as Pastor Kind caught him.

"Quiet," the pastor bellowed, and the boy started crying. Dingo Boots moved forward again and lifted the little boy onto the altar that sat in the middle of the raised platform. He struggled, trying to release his arms from their grip, but the man held him down.

Val almost yelled but stopped herself and just growled to Cam, "Fuck! Is this some kind of sick child sacrifice?"

"I don't know what they're up to, but your mom figured it out. That's why she wrote down their next moves and then hid the list."

"They must have found out that she knew something and needed to see if she had evidence."

"Or maybe they knew she had the list."

Pastor Kind bellowed again, and they both jumped. "The rapture of youth is the closest to perfect rapture! Get the camera, Nedra! We need a witness!"

The girl from the accident set up a tripod and helped Nedra attach a small digital video camera to it. Val was so engrossed with watching them that she didn't see what was happening at the altar until Cam nudged her.

Val's stomach turned as Mack unbuttoned the little boy's shirt. She felt like she was going to throw up.

"Oh, God," she said, swallowing back foul bile. She turned to Cam suddenly. "The video camera at Mack's. The lemonade dispenser was for kids only so he could get them to go pee. But it wasn't just him. All of these people are involved. This is some sort of child-pornography *cult*. Jesus—"

The little boy screamed, and Val turned back to see Pastor Kind struggling with the boy, who was fighting to keep his pants on.

Val took off running, her legs pumping as fast as they could, and reached the front door of the church. She pulled roughly on the handle, but it was locked.

Cam caught up with her. "Val, wait!"

"For what?"

"We've got to get the police!"

"Fuck that. We don't have time."

She raced back around to the window where they'd watched the horrific events, and Val could hear Cam's footsteps behind her. She skidded to a stop and dove into the bushes by the window.

She heard Cam whisper loudly, "What are you doing?" but couldn't answer. She grabbed what she was looking for, jerked the big rock up over her head, and threw it at the window. It crashed through, flinging the drapes aside and spewing shards of glass into the sanctuary.

Screams erupted from inside and Pastor Kind yelled something.

Val grabbed Cam's arm, pulling her. "Now let's go get the police."

She and Cam turned just as Mack yelled, "It's Cam and Val!"

"Get your car keys ready," Val said as they ran around toward the front of the church. Sprinting as fast as she could, she jabbed a hand into her pants pocket to get her phone. She had to call 911. But when she pulled it out, it slipped from her hand and crashed onto the pavement on the side of the building. She tried to stop but slid and came down hard on her hip. Cam grunted loudly and almost tumbled over her. She scrambled over, grabbed the phone, and pushed back up to her feet.

As they rounded the church and came out in front, Donna and all the men in the group were already dashing out. Pastor Kind was in the lead, and Val could tell that they could easily cut them off before they reached the car.

Val stopped quickly and reversed direction, running back toward the side of the church. She was still trying to unlock her phone but couldn't afford to lose precious seconds by slowing down to look and dial.

They reached the corner of the building, and in a split second Val realized Cam hadn't said a word since she'd broken the window. And while her mind processed the possible reasons—was she in too much shock or were things not going as planned, whatever that plan might be—she heard the little boy scream again.

Impulse took over and she took off, heading around the back. She got to the window and looked behind her. Cam hadn't followed. She grabbed the edge of the side frame, scrambling up the wall, and leapt up on the sill and through the opening. A sharp pain tore at her knee as she grabbed one side of the drapes and lowered herself into the sanctuary.

Nedra started, grabbing the child from the altar and pulling him down violently. He bellowed again, crying out in a wail that Val had only heard once before from a gravely injured sheep, hit by a car and bawling as it lay on a farm road.

Val ran toward Nedra, but her leg buckled and a hot knife of pain twisted around her kneecap. She groaned and grabbed the end of a pew, pulling herself closer.

"Val! Stop!" Nedra yelled. Her face was red with fury.

Val grabbed the last pew and ignored the agony in her knee, loping as fast as she could. She'd balled a fist, readying it for Nedra's face, when a rough tug pulled her to the left. The girl from the accident held onto her shirt, dragging her toward the opposite pew. Val tried to dig her heels into the carpet but her knee wouldn't work, so she deliberately fell forward, knocking the girl onto the wooden pew. She heard a loud crack as the girl's side connected with the seat, and in the second her grip slipped, Val hit her face, sending the delinquent to the floor.

Val turned back toward Nedra, focused only on getting to the boy.

Nedra was dragging him by his arm, trying to pull him toward the back of the room. Val's knee felt like it was exploding, but getting to the little boy was more important. She hobbled, using her good leg to thrust herself farther forward.

The boy kicked and flailed against Nedra's grasp, which slowed them down enough for Val to catch up. She got up on the platform, passed the altar, and reached Nedra, who was now at the entrance to a back hallway.

She reached out and grabbed Nedra's hair, pulling her down as hard as she could. The woman dropped and so did the little boy. Nedra answered with a swift backhand to Val's cheek, and she stumbled backward. The little boy seemed completely terrified, and his high-pitched screams echoed off the acoustic wall panels that were designed to help people praise God, not abuse children. Val shook off the sharp pain, and her anger suddenly peaked.

Grunting loudly, Nedra began scooting backward on her butt, pulling the boy into the hallway. She scrambled to her feet and jerked the boy up with her. Val grabbed Nedra's blouse and pushed her roughly against the wall, moving between Nedra and the door.

Nedra's face was bloodred, and she almost hissed when she spoke. "Val, this is none of your business."

"I know what this is all about. Let him go."

"Get out of my way."

Val didn't care that Nedra's eyes looked as if they'd turned to steel and her expression was washed in some kind of manic insanity.

"Go, you fucking bitch, but not with the boy."

"They'll be back and they'll kill you, Val. Get out of my way."

"You're already in deep shit. Leave him."

Nedra raised her voice. "Get out of my way."

Val stood her ground as Nedra's eyes darted back and forth, obviously looking for another way out. The woman began to shake, her face quivering as if her head were about to burst. Her stare was beyond menacing. "You, OUT!"

This needs to be over now, Val thought. The idea of them abusing this poor little boy, frightened out of his mind, enraged her like nothing else in her life ever had.

"No," she said as she dropped her fist back behind her. "*You*, out."

Val brought her fist around, throwing her shoulder into the inertia, and connected with Nedra's face with such force the woman's head snapped to the right. She smacked into the wall and crumpled to the floor.

Val yowled at the hot pain throbbing in her hand and shook it quickly before holding it out to the boy.

"Let's get you home," she said, grateful when he didn't fight her.

They rushed down the hallway and found a side door. She pushed him out into the night and led him around toward the front.

When they reached the corner, she slowed and stopped, squatting down next to him. "Are you okay?"

He was still crying but otherwise only nodded.

"What's your name, honey?"

"Edgar Santorino. I live at 44 Crest Drive."

His response sounded like something his parents had made him memorize.

"Okay, Edgar. We're going to get you home. But right now, I don't know where the other bad guys are, so I need you to stay right here while I go take a look."

Before she could stand, Edgar threw his arms around her and hugged her as if he were drowning in the ocean.

Her heart broke into a million pieces. "It's okay. You're okay," she said.

He let her go and she put a finger to her mouth, motioning him to be quiet. "Be right back."

Edging up to the corner, Val leaned out so she could peek around to the front.

Donna and the men were in the parking lot, and she could see that they'd encircled Cam. Val was too far away to hear them talking, but they were in a fierce discussion.

Val couldn't simply march out there with the boy and demand they let Cam go. She also didn't have the car keys to drive the boy away. Maybe she could get the boy to the car and have him wait there until she could somehow get Cam to make a run for it.

She was just about to turn back to the boy when Donna stepped toward Cam and put her arms around her. She began whispering something in her ear.

Cam was so close to Donna, listening to whatever she was saying. The men stood there and watched. Then she saw Cam nod, and Val suddenly spun away, falling against the side of the building. Her ears began to buzz and her stomach threatened to heave everything out of her.

There it was, the horrible truth playing out right before her eyes. They were planning their next move. And Cam was in on all of it.

A nauseating dizziness threatened to topple her. She steadied herself against the wall. Tears welled up in her eyes and she held her breath, trying not to lose it right where she stood.

The distant sound of sirens made her pause. When she knew they were approaching, and before she completely lost her ability to function, she limped back to the boy. She had to sneak him out through the woods and find a house where she could call 911.

CHAPTER EIGHTEEN

Holding a cup of coffee she hadn't touched in a half an hour, Val sat at her mother's dining-room table, staring at the grain of the wooden top. The tree rings looked like little roads running circles around themselves. That's how her life had gone lately. She had no control of the events happening around her and was just running in circles, reacting to whatever transpired.

And the night before had been the final spin, the last road for Val on this strange trip back to her childhood home.

Her head pounded as if she'd enjoyed a night of revelry and alcohol-infused merriment, but the extremely hung-over feeling, and the matching sour stomach, had had no happy origins.

The long night had been brutal. She flip-flopped between crying about Cam and crying for her mom. When sleep had failed her, she finally got out of bed around five that morning.

Coffee had always provided comfort and smelled so good to her, but that morning she couldn't even lift the mug to her lips. It seemed as if her hands had become a dead weight. Like a deserted road that no one ever uses to get to their destination, the connection between her brain and whatever motor neurons were supposed to reach the muscle fibers of her hand were now broken down and forsaken. She was spent and completely destroyed.

That Cam would not only pretend to care about her being victimized and injured, but would take part in the plot, hurt her beyond description.

Val had come back to town to take care of the business of death. She had simply needed to get everything done and then head back home to grieve in peace. But people who had their own horrible agenda and possessed no empathy for a dead mother and her daughter had blown that plan to shit.

Val had snuck little Edgar away from the church and through the woods to a small house that was tidy and well kept. Thankfully, the woman who answered was kind and accepting. She'd called the police and offered Val and the boy water while they waited. They sat on a settee that looked like it came from a farm, and the rest of the room was comfortably decorated with things you'd expect a grandmotherly type to have. A white hutch housed her display of china, and a dark-brown throw rug complemented the delicate beige lace curtains that hung in the windows.

Edgar clung to Val and didn't say much except to repeat that he lived at 44 Crest Drive. Val kept a firm, protective arm around him to let him know that no more bad things would happen to him that night.

Val told the woman a little about why they'd fled the church but kept it rather vague for the sake of the boy. She wasn't sure how much he understood of what had really happened and didn't want to make his nightmare worse.

By the look of shock on the woman's face, she seemed to have no idea what had been going on at The Seeds of Light church. And whether she was prejudiced by the mention of bad things or just motivated to add to the talk, she seemed to know a lot about the church and wasn't a fan at all. She said it seemed like a strange place, with over-zealous parishioners. She expressed a disdain for the music that drifted through the trees and bothered her peaceful Sundays and evenings and didn't trust any church that wasn't "Catholic, Jewish, or any of the other main ones."

When a police officer arrived, he put them in a squad car and offered to take her to the hospital to get her knee looked at. She declined, so he drove them to the station. In all the years Val had previously lived in Hemlock, she'd never seen the inside of the building. It was very normal looking and what she would expect for a small-town combination city hall and police headquarters. The lobby walls were paneled, and the floor had worn linoleum tiles that were checkered with chocolate-brown and beige. The wood desk matched the paneling, and it all reminded Val of her high school's main office.

They were led back to an interview room. Edgar looked afraid so Val made small talk with him until an officer came back in, telling them they'd located Edgar's parents. He said he wanted to get Val's statement while they waited for Edgar's parents to arrive.

Val thought the boy had been through enough. She asked to be taken to a different room to make her statement, but Edgar tugged on her hand. He chirped out a "no," reminding her of a helpless little bird. He looked so small, sitting on the metal interrogation chair, that Val relented.

She told the officer what she'd seen at the church. She told them she'd suspected something was about to happen and that she'd gone there, detailing what she saw and how she made a commotion to stop them from molesting Edgar.

"How did you come to suspect something?" the officer asked.

Val pulled the note out of her pocket. "My mother left this before she died. I figured out what the numbers meant." She decoded it for him.

"And how did your mother know to write this down?"

Val shrugged. "I don't know. She was a member of the church and must have found out about it."

"I'm going to need a copy of that note."

"Did they arrest them all?" Val said, nervous that Mack might have taken off and was running free.

"The call we responded to was for a fight in the church parking lot."

"And?"

"We arrested two people."

"Who? Which ones?"

"Mack and Cam."

"But they're all involved in this." She pointed to Edgar. "All of them."

"If that's true, we'll round up the rest of them. But we have to conduct an investigation first to see what evidence there is."

❖

Val looked down at the coffee mug in her hand, and memories of her mom, always up before she arose, as well as the aroma of freshly brewing java, came back easily. As a child, sometimes she could filter out her mother's boyfriends as well as the instances when Val was more in the way than not. During those times, she'd fantasized about a world where it was just she and her mom, eating breakfast and planning the day together, with no one waking up later, barking for food, and then slapping her mom on the ass when he sauntered into the kitchen.

Now her mother's house felt so much emptier than it ever had.

She spent the morning contacting real-estate agents who might be able to take over the listing. Most seemed more interested in why she was dumping Nedra Tobias than asking about Val's particular needs. She imagined the local realty world would explode when the reigning real-estate agent's true identity was revealed. They would run out of their open houses and raise their for-sale signs in celebration of the fall of the wicked queen. If Nedra had dominated the town's housing sales like she intimated, the realtor serfs would rejoice around the village well and individually plan the siege of her castle.

Val hadn't felt good about any of the agents, so she gave up on Hemlock and made some calls to realtors in the towns to the south. She finally found one who asked the right questions and didn't care about the queen and her queendom. Val made an appointment to meet with her the next day.

Val had spent the last hour or so on the phone and not thinking about Cam. But the respite brought her only slight relief because, as soon as finished her last call, her stomach went stale and she was back in the sadness she'd woken up with.

She walked slowly back into the kitchen. Her ribs were finally feeling better, but the gash she'd received at the church burned hot in her joint. She'd fashioned a butterfly bandage to close the skin, and it was holding pretty well, but the sum of the cuts and bruises on every rib, her knees, and her forehead hurt only a fraction as much as the pain she felt at Cam's betrayal.

Val leaned over the sink and grabbed a sponge to clean the coffee pot.

Cam was the pariah of Hemlock. Shouldn't that have been a clue?

Mr. Harlin liked Cam, though. He was her chief supporter. But he only knew her from her candy deliveries. What did he know about who she really was? He didn't venture out much, and what could he really learn about her if he saw her in only one particular context?

She scrubbed the inside of the glass pot, talking out loud to no one. "You had this all thought out, didn't you, Cam? The whole 'let me help you figure out the clues' routine deserves a standing ovation. The way you figured out what the catapult thing was… genius, Cam. And I have to hand it to Donna for trying to convince me I should stay away from you. I have to admit the pitiful fact that your reverse-psychology shit really worked on me, didn't it?

"And Cam, your whole performance was truly award winning. Tell me, how did you keep such a straight face when I told you about getting beaten up? How easy was it to tell me you liked me, huh?"

She pushed the sponge harder and harder into the coffee pot as she counted off the things Cam had said to her.

"Why don't you come by and I'll make you some special chocolate turtles?" Val said, plunging the sponge into the pot. "Oh, and 'I'm glad you're glad that I'm gay.' Christ on a crutch."

The pot was taking a beating. "'Are you sure you're feeling all right?'" Val remembered Cam's bogus concern, and added, "'after being almost *gassed* to death?'"

But Cam had truly taken her well-acted role too far when they'd made love in Mr. Harlin's car. When she thought about how vulnerable Cam had made her feel, she thrust her hand back in the pot, punching it so hard it shattered. Pieces of glass exploded in the sink, and she jerked her hand away as she dropped the handle onto the shards.

She rested her elbows on the edge of the sink, her hands dropping in, and began to cry. The ache of betrayal was so intense her chest stung as if a thousand livid bees had attacked her. The debris in the sink became blurry, and she surrendered again to the deluge of tears that needed to come.

"God damn her." She was now blubbering. "Damn you and fuck you, Cam."

She cried out, letting her wails release the total and utter indignities she'd been subjected to. Her nose ran and she didn't care. She wanted to purge every feeling from her body until she had nothing left to cry over. She needed to exorcise the stench of Cam's duplicity and purge herself of the memories that had once felt so damn good.

"Get out," she whimpered, repeating and repeating the command until her sobs slowed and her crying stopped.

When the kitchen became quiet again, Val blinked the last of the tears from her eyes.

"Shit," she said, noticing a fairly significant amount of blood in the sink, pooled around the glass, with streaks that had escaped down the drain. She turned her hand over and saw that two of her knuckles had been sliced. "Shit God damn mother*FUCKER*," she yelled, and ripped a few sheets of paper towel off the roll on the counter. She turned to lean her butt against the sink and pressed the towel to her hand.

Her cell phone rang, so she walked over to the dining-room table where she'd left it. Gripping her right hand with paper towels, she leaned over to see the screen. It was from a local number she didn't recognize. She poked the screen to answer and set it to speakerphone.

"Hello?"

A bland-sounding recording spoke. "An inmate is calling collect from the Hemlock City Jail. To accept, please press 'one' on your phone."

Val froze as a sudden tornado of emotions spun inside her. Anger, betrayal, disappointment, and even desire whirled around like chairs and cars and house parts slamming into her in an Oklahoma storm.

Was she ready to confront her? What would Cam say? Would Val's mouth even work, or would her throat seize up and strangle any words that she tried to use to describe what was spiraling around deeper inside her?

The message repeated.

She wanted to cry, but she didn't have any tears left to purge. She reached down and pushed the "end call" button.

Chapter Nineteen

Val finished bandaging her knuckles, though it took forever to get them to stop bleeding. She found some gauze and folded it up in small squares, then taped them onto her knuckles with a few Band-Aids to absorb as much blood as she could.

It was hard for her to bend her fingers, but what the hell did she care?

All she had to do was meet with the new realtor and arrange to have her mother's things liquidated. In between calls to realtors, she'd found a Portland company that would come out and hold an estate sale for her. They'd take a percentage and send her a check for the rest. That way, she could leave town right away and be done with Hemlock and everyone in it.

She walked into the living room and sat on the couch. Looking around the room, she mentally inventoried what she wanted to take before her mother's things were dispersed to Lord knows who to be reused or resold or eventually go in the trash.

So, that was about it. Remove any valuables, sell the house, sell the car, and never return to Hemlock.

Oh, and more than likely be available sometime in the future to testify or whatever she'd have to do when a trial was set for the porn-ring group. That meant a return trip.

She imagined it might be a long time before she got her mother's car back since it was still at Mack's. With him in jail, she was sure the business was closed or at least not running the way it had.

Maybe she'd have to arrange for a tow truck to pick it up and haul it to some other garage. Or maybe she should just leave it where it sat.

Perhaps she'd tow it to a vacant parking lot and put a sign on it that read FOR SALE: DEER ACCIDENT—DEEPLY DISCOUNTED. Better yet, it should read FOR SALE: VICTIM OF A PORNO RING, SMASHED UP AS BAD AS MY HEART WAS.

She could arrange for the car to be picked up without her even setting foot in that horrible place. The thought that the camera was probably still mounted above the toilet disgusted her. That he was targeting children, tempting them to drink all the lemonade they wanted and then recording them…

Val shook her head as if she'd just swallowed a putrid piece of meat.

But would the police find the camera? Surely neither Nedra nor anyone else in that group would reveal its existence. If they did know, they'd definitely get a search warrant and discover the tapes in Mack's office, then tie them to the horrible things going on at the church.

When she'd spoken to the police, she hadn't said anything about Cam and her being in the garage. She had left out important details and would probably be charged with withholding evidence, because they had broken in, for God sakes.

She paused at the realization that she'd committed a crime. Of course, she knew she had all along, but now that the others were in jail and Val wanted to spit on all of their graves, she needed to admit that she wasn't without reproach herself.

She kicked at the leg of the coffee table.

"Cam's probably already told the police I broke into Mack's twice," she said, reasoning aloud because she hoped it would help straighten out this new wrinkle a little. "But something was way off, and I wanted to see what they were doing to my car. And yes, I could have waited until the garage opened to go, but something told me I couldn't trust anything that was going on."

She looked up, as if a detective were standing in front of her. "Sure. Yeah, I broke in. But I'm not a frickin' pervert. I had no idea what they were doing. I just knew that Mack had something to do with the attempts on my life."

She kicked the leg of the coffee table again. "So I get charged with it, so what."

But as soon as she said that, her heart jumped. "Fuck," she said. "Fuck!"

Blood was seeping through the bandages around her knuckles. She made a fist, which hurt like hell, but she didn't give a shit.

Out the dining-room window, the pine trees looked so stoic and serene. She wished she were a child again, standing in the front yard, inhaling the comforting pine scent. As long as that woodsy fragrance surrounded her she would be fine.

But she wasn't.

A car turned off Coast Highway and she recognized it right away. Mr. Harlin's Gran Torino pulled up to Val's house and parked.

Mr. Harlin took his time exiting the car, holding on to the doorframe and then the roof of the car while he closed the door, his movements very deliberate and careful, as if he were anticipating an earthquake. He carried a paper bag as he walked slowly up the walkway, and Val got up from her chair. Her knee was swollen and hurt like a mother, so she walked slowly, opening the door for him as he reached the bottom step.

"Mr. Harlin," she said.

"I'm sorry to bother you, but could you spare a few minutes?"

Val stood aside to let him in. "Of course."

She directed him to the table and went to fetch him a cup of tea since she'd just broken her coffee pot. When she returned, one of the VHS tapes, the metal plate, and the spring from Mack's garage lay on the table in front of him.

"Thank you," he said, and took the mug from her. "Cam told me if anything happened to her to take this to the police. The plate and spring, I mean. And the tape," he said. "There's only the one there, because I destroyed the other. It had you on it. I watched them until I found you. No one will ever know of its existence.

"That tape there, though," he pointed to it, "will make you want to throw up, but by God, it's evidence to take that sinner down." He nodded toward the table but Val was already staring at the pieces, the first stirrings of anger roiling around in her gut.

"Why are you telling me this?" Val said.

"I think you should do it. Take these things to the police."

"Why me?"

"Because while you're there, Cam will want to see you."

"Why would I do that?"

He looked at her and blinked rapidly in what looked like surprise.

"Mr. Harlin, Cam was in on the whole thing from the beginning—the gas incident here at the house, the beating I got from Mack's men. Cam pretended not to know anything about all that, but she did know."

Mr. Harlin tilted his head and gave her the strangest stare. "Cam," he said slowly. "She got beaten up pretty badly at the church last night. I know the janitor at the jail, and he told me. They're going to charge her in the child-pornography ring."

Val was emphatic yet trying not to raise her voice. "I saw her talking to Donna, Mr. Harlin. Cam was with the whole group, and she and Donna were whispering something. If she wasn't in on it, would she be having a special, private moment with a woman who abuses children for money?" Val knew her fingers were tapping the tabletop a little too forcefully, but staying angry made her feel much less vulnerable. "She duped me into trusting her so they could get the evidence my mother had against them."

"That doesn't make sense."

A snicker escaped Val's mouth. "None of this has made any sense, Mr. Harlin. But I saw what I saw."

"I don't know what you thought you saw, but Cam wouldn't do any of that. She's not that way."

"Can you know for sure? Nedra seemed like a pillar of this town, and look what she ended up being. Cam was a troublemaker in high school. I was there, I saw it. Sometimes the apple doesn't fall far from its own tree."

"Cam went to jail once," Mr. Harlin said.

"I know. She told me. She broke some windows at the high school."

"Did she tell you her brother actually did it? She took the blame because she was afraid if he went to jail for it, he'd never get over the stigma. She knew they were better than that, but he was too sensitive. So she protected him and did the time instead.

"And she made restitution. She worked every job she could find to pay back the school. And she kept working until she could afford to send her brother to college in Seattle. She made sure he got out of this town because he never would have had a chance here. Because of that, she was stuck here all these years, suffering the name-calling and discrimination, but she rose above it and became a respectable businesswoman. And a good friend to me. And to you."

Mr. Harlin put his hand on the table and used it to stand up. He shuffled away from the chair. "Sometimes," he said when Val stood, "if you look down on people, you lose the opportunity to help them up."

He ambled out of the dining room and Val walked with him, opening the front door for him.

He turned to her and said, "For the Lord sees not as man sees: man looks on the outward appearance, but the Lord looks on the heart." He bowed slightly, as if thanking her for her time. "That's the first book of Samuel, 16:7."

She watched him stroll to his car and made sure he got in okay. He turned toward her as he started the engine. Val waved but realized her gesture was as tired and uncertain as she felt.

Who was Cam, really? And why should she trust one old man?

The bigger question was, why had she let herself get pulled into this mess? Why hadn't she just taken care of her business and left town instead of playing some older and dumber version of Nancy Drew? If she'd been smarter, she would have never broken the law or allowed Cam access to her heart.

Why had she taken it so damn far?

And then, it was as if something or someone made her turn her head. Her gaze landed on the dining-room table where the metal piece and the spring still sat. Reaching into her pocket, she pulled out the key. She'd kept it with her since she and Cam had found it.

And she had her answer.

CHAPTER TWENTY

"Wait here," a police officer instructed her. She sat on a metal chair across from another chair. A wall of bars separated the two. Cement cinder blocks made up the rest of the small room. They were painted white as if somehow the lightness of the color would brighten the ambiance of the room, but signs stating multiple restrictions ruined the effort. No cell phones. No contraband. No loud, abusive, or obscene language. No excessive kissing, touching, and/or grooming.

Val's hands shook as she tried to calm herself. It was a risk to show up at a police station that might be looking for her, but she was equally nervous about seeing Cam. She didn't want to be here but she had questions. And she would demand answers.

Cam was brought in through a series of barred doors. She was wearing a dark-blue smock and draw-string pants, but they were barely in the same color range as the bottoms, being at least four bleach shades lighter than the top. Val attempted to control her breathing as Cam passed through the last door. While the police officer instructed her about something, Cam kept her head down, looking only at the floor, which gave Val a chance to blow a few breaths out, readying herself for the confrontation.

Cam looked awful. Her body slumped over slightly, maybe from the burden of her circumstances or maybe from the guilt of her actions, but it wasn't until she turned toward her and looked up that Val saw the real source of her demeanor.

Her face had been brutalized. Her eyes were black and were probably both bloodshot, but only one eye could open up at all. Her lip was split, and her left cheek was so swollen, it could have easily been broken. She had inflamed, dark-red scrapes across the right side of her face, and Val could tell by the parallel streaks that they came from being dragged along pavement of some kind.

Val grew nauseous, and the pain of her recent beating came right back to her. She winced, as if actually feeling Cam's wounds.

The officer nodded and Cam walked toward Val. When she got to the chair and sat, she finally looked up. They were less than two feet apart, with a short table between them divided vertically by jail bars. Cam's cheeks were swollen, and her forehead had dried blood from a few cuts that ran lengthwise across her hairline. One eye was swollen shut and the other was bloodshot. Her lip had been split open as well. Val was still so shocked by Cam's horribly beaten face she lost whatever words she'd decided to say to her.

"Did the police do this to you?"

Cam furrowed her eyebrows. "No." She seemed confused.

"Who did?"

"Mack." Cam gingerly ran her tongue over a cut in her swollen bottom lip. "And those guys."

"What are you talking about?"

"They beat the shit out of me."

"They—"

"I don't understand, Val. Why didn't you come to the jail last night?"

"I did. I was here being questioned by the police." Val was becoming just as confused. And the more she looked at Cam's face, both eyes gooped up with some sort of medicinal ointment, just seeing the amount of injury and pain made Val's own eyes water in response.

"When I went behind the church," Val said, "you didn't follow me. You went back out to your friends, didn't you?"

"You were running back behind the church, and I knew you were going to try to help that little boy. I didn't want them to stop you so I ran back out to the parking lot, hoping they'd chase me instead of you. I was trying to lead them away from the church and past the parking lot, but they caught me and dragged me over to their cars."

"I saw you, Cam. You and Donna were standing close," Val said, her stomach sour with the memory, "and whispering in each other's ears."

Cam's open eye narrowed and then closed a moment as she lowered her head. "She was threatening me," she said, looking back up again. "She whispered in my ear that if I didn't shut up about what I saw, Mack would make sure I was never found again. She told me that even if I did say something, no one in town would believe me anyway. And that my past would guarantee it. She said they'd find you and finish what they started and that this time the house would explode with you in it." She hesitated and dug her fingers into the table in front of her. "She told me that the boys would probably rape you first, though, just for fun.

"Then she tried to reason with me and sweet-talk me since we'd been lovers once. She said that instead of all that, I could choose to go along with it. They'd pay me to keep quiet and even give me a percentage of the profits from their enterprise if I kept my mouth shut.

"And what you saw when I whispered back was me telling her to shove it up her ass like Mack probably liked to do. I also told her that if any of those assholes even touched you one more time, I'd kill every last one of them. That's when I got pummeled."

Val was stunned. This was the last thing she'd expected Cam to say. She only had her gut to go by, and while Cam's outward actions up until the night before had been consistent and seemingly sincere, did she really know Cam at all?

Val was the outsider, the new stranger in town, the mark. And while it was indisputable that Nedra and Mack and the rest had deliberately gone after her to protect their sick venture, had Cam been the insider? Was she the magician's shill in the naive audience of one? And if she wasn't, how was Val supposed to just believe her?

"If that's true, why did you get arrested and not just Mack?"

"When the police got there, Nedra and Pastor Kind said that I started the fight." She laughed but sounded pitiful. "I told them Mack and the other two assholes had beaten me, so they decided to take us both in."

"And let the others go?"

Cam looked as disappointed as Val felt. "Yeah."

"Well," Val said. Things were beginning to make a bit more sense. If Cam had been in on the whole mess, Mack wouldn't have beaten her up. "The fact that I got to this room without being arrested tells me that you haven't said anything about me."

"Why would I? You're the victim here."

Val looked at the woman she'd spent the last few days with. She was the woman who'd reached out to her, helped her, and made love to her. All the things that encouraged trust. Val had spent her life wary of pretty much everyone. She truly sucked at trusting people, but Cam had opened a door, and, for the first time, Val had walked in with open arms.

"Why did you pursue this with me, Cam? If you're telling the truth, you took a big chance when you met me. Until you stepped in, you didn't have anything to do with this and could have walked away from it all."

"You needed help."

"Most of the town thinks you're the person who'd do exactly what we did at the garage. But you tell me that you've spent years working hard to erase that reputation."

"I know what I've done and haven't done," She jerked her head back slightly to the jail cells behind her, and Val presumed she was indicating Nedra and the rest. "I'm not sure I'll ever convince people of who I really am, but I had a chance to help substantiate the fact that Hemlock has some real villains. They're the worst kind, too. They wear their upright citizen's faces all day, get us to trust them, but they're the worst, most despicable human beings imaginable.

"I also got to know you and wanted to help you, no matter what you needed. That's probably a fault of mine. Maybe I don't know when to stop, but I didn't want to stop with you. You needed someone to help you because everything seemed confusing and fucked up. You needed someone you could trust."

"Yeah, I know about trust, Cam. Especially how it can be stomped on and flung around like some abused alley cat."

Cam's eye began to water and she folded her hands together, clenching them until her knuckles turned white.

"I regret so many things right now," Cam said. "We should have gone to the police long before last night. I shouldn't have taken you back to the garage the second time. And I'm so sorry I couldn't keep you from getting hurt by those people, Val. But most of all, I'm sorry you're in so much pain right now. I can't make you believe me. All I can do is tell you I'm so, so sorry."

Val inhaled a ragged breath full of overwhelming emotions. She was hurt and tired and confused. And she was crazy about Cam. She'd never before felt so exposed, and it terrified her.

But what scared her even more was the thought of getting up and walking away from this jail and never being with Cam again. When she'd first seen her, so badly beaten, her face so broken by the fists of those horrible men, her doubt about Cam had started to crumble.

Of course it made sense that Cam would try to fend them off for her. She was a protector.

She'd protected her brother from a life she'd already been sentenced to and spent her life fighting the swift and relentless current of Hemlock's cruel prejudice and small-minded judgment. And then she'd reached out to shelter and protect Val. The proof that Cam had been telling the truth about that night at the church had been horribly battered into her face.

"I wanted to leave town this morning. Leave and never come back," Val said. She pulled the key from her pocket and held it up. "But my mom left this. I believe she was asking me to do something with it. I believe she'd found out what Nedra was doing and was planning to go to the police. She made that list, locked it away in a safe place, and then hid the key in a place that only two people knew about.

"But then she died and," Val paused, swallowing back the wretched sadness that hung in her throat, "I think I was supposed to help her finish this. There were so many things I should have done and didn't. But she gave me one more chance, and I needed to take it.

"Mom could have written me off long ago," she said. "My actions and my outward appearance told her I didn't care anymore, but she knew that in my heart I was still her daughter. And she was right." So was Mr. Harlin, she thought. "She saw my heart, not my actions.

"And I saw that in you, Cam. I was exposed and defenseless, but you held out your hand to me. I took it and it felt so wonderful. I'm not good at trusting, I never have been, so when I saw you at the church with Donna, I just spun out.

"Nevertheless, I want to trust your heart, Cam. It scares the hell out of me, but I know now that outward appearances aren't the whole truth. And I know you aren't the bad person this town thinks you are."

Cam was crying harder now. She looked so small in that oversized jail outfit. At that moment, Val knew that it was safe to trust her. Of all the people that she'd never completely allowed in, here was an ex-juvenile delinquent who'd turned out to be her true liberator. She found in being with Cam the desire to throw caution into the nearby ocean and let the waves pulverize it.

Even though Cam's hands were still clenched together, they shook, and Val wished she could reach out and hold her. But she couldn't do that. Not just yet. There was, however, something she could do.

"Cam, hang in there a little longer. I need to go make this all right."

Cam looked at her with such feeling that Val knew it wasn't a lie. Her heart strained to break free from its cage of bones and flesh and pour out all the love it held for Cam.

"I will be back. Believe me."

❖

Val met with a Hemlock detective named Randall and handed him the bag Mr. Harlin had brought over earlier that day.

She told him everything, as it had happened. Detective Randall took copious notes, stopping every once in a while to give her a look. She couldn't tell what was behind his expression, but it was either incredulity at the crazy events he was hearing about or frustration because he was now going to have to transcribe all of it into what would surely be a lengthy report.

She admitted she'd broken into Mack's garage and that the tapes came from his office. She also added that she hadn't revealed that part to the police the night before because she knew it would implicate her.

"But I don't care any longer what happens to me," she told the detective. "I broke in because I knew something bad was happening. If I get into trouble because of it, it's okay. Those people had to stop what they were doing."

"The officer who took your statement last night said you're Kris Montague's kid."

"I am," Val said.

"She was a hell of a nice lady."

"That was nice of you to say, Detective Randall."

His nod seemed reverent, which meant a lot to her.

"What happens now that I've told you about breaking into the garage?"

The detective tapped his pen on the notebook. It made a deadened, thudding sound that Val likened to the second hand of a clock, ticking toward an answer that might be really bad.

"We'll need to conduct an investigation first. You admitted breaking in, so you'll probably face charges." For the first time that day, he looked at her differently. Gone was the lackluster but dubious expression of a police officer who wasn't quite sure what to believe. In its place was an unexpected affability of sorts. "But I'm not going to detain you tonight. If there really turns out to be a child-pornography ring, and the evidence shows it, the district attorney's office may decide to drop your burglary charge. They may cite that, in the interest of justice, it was for a reasonable cause. It doesn't happen often, but it could. And if that fails, judges have been known to dismiss cases for the same reason."

"You mean for the way I collected the evidence?"

"Yes. But hear me when I say that you broke the law. There are no guarantees. You should talk to a lawyer."

The reality of her actions sobered her faster than a naked plunge in an ice pond. She didn't want to be arrested for burglary, but she had broken in. The frightened face of little Edgar when he'd almost been accosted made her own fear dissipate quickly. Those bastards had to be stopped.

"Thank you, Detective."

"And stick around. No flying back home unless you talk to us first," Detective Randall said as he sat back and looked at the tape, metal plate, and spring sitting on the table in front of them. "Deer catapult, gas leak—that's a wild story, you know."

"I do. And I never thought it'd lead to all this."

He got up and said, "Wait here."

Just outside the open door, the detective spoke with another officer. "Call Judge Turner and get a warrant for Mack's place. It's about the child-porn report from last night. Looks like we have evidence in his office."

Val waited until he returned and sat down. "There's something else I need to tell you."

"Oh, boy."

"It's about Cam Nelson. She's being held because of the fight last night at the church."

He nodded.

"The same group I told you about."

"Okay."

"She's not part of them. She was with me when I went to the church. She tried to stop them. When I got the boy out of there, they caught her in the parking lot. They knew we'd found out what they were doing so they beat her up. She needs to be released. She had nothing to do with them."

"You know who Cam Nelson is, don't you?"

"If you're referring to her reputation, I'm aware of the gossip. All I'm saying is that she's not part of that child-porn stuff. They beat her up because they knew she'd go to the police."

He seemed to chew on that information for a minute. "We've got two things going on here: the he-said-she-said fight last night and separate allegations about what happened to Edgar Santorino. You say she's not guilty of either offense." He stood up and collected his notebook. "We'll look into both."

"Thank you." She felt a little relief that maybe Cam wouldn't have to stay behind bars much longer.

Detective Randall aimed his pen toward his shirt's front chest pocket and slid it in. "Remember, don't go anywhere."

Val got into her rental car and left the Hemlock Police Station.

The day's fog had long since burned off and the people of the little beach town were going about their business, soon to become very aware of the newest scandal. This one, with such topics as child porn, Pastor Kind, and Nedra Tobias, would surely be a doozy.

She drove up her mother's street, pulled into the driveway, and parked. Nedra's sign still stood out front, but a new real-estate agent would be taking it down and replacing it with a new one. Nedra would, in effect, be removed from her life, and that would be a very good thing. She got out of her car and walked across the grass to the walkway. Stopping at the foot of the steps to the front door, she faced Coast Highway and closed her eyes.

As she inhaled deeply, she smelled the salty air from eons of fish and sand and kelp. It was a never-ending reminder that the sea, and all its sublime beauty, was both peaceful and turbulent, both myth and tradition. Hemlock was the same way. The peaceful little town had a tempestuous vein of malevolence, and the fairy tale that was advertised had darker rituals that had sullied its traditions.

Hemlock had lost some of its innocence but, for the most part, would certainly recover and live to boast about its noteworthy and distinct latitude marker and celebrate another tourist season.

The 45th parallel was both something and nothing, depending on how one looked at it. For Val, it had been an exact middle ground where she'd been forced to the edge.

When Val had originally booked her flight to Oregon, she'd planned a short visit to Hemlock, but what had actually occurred was a long trip down a strange road. The experience wasn't unlike her first night's drive back into town. Coast Highway was dark and foreboding, full of potholes and curves, and a terrible, unexpected detour.

But when Cam had come into the picture, everything had changed. Val now knew she couldn't just leave town and be done with Hemlock. She had to see this through, no matter what that meant. She had to help Cam get out of jail. And she needed, more than anything, to feel her in her arms again.

CHAPTER TWENTY-ONE

The police moved rather quickly. At least that's what the local paper was reporting. Val would have sworn the President of the United States had murdered the Secretary of State for all the press Nedra and her clan received. Of course, all the Oregon papers and news stations were covering the arrests and subsequent disgraces, but Val spent the next few days enjoying the rich and lively updates from the *Hemlock Sea Scroll* the most. The reporters were not only mining every detail they could quarry from the rich mountains that were the lives of Nedra Tobias and Pastor Kind; they were also far from neutral in their coverage.

The police had quickly gotten the search warrant on Mack's garage and found the rest of the tapes exactly where Cam had told her they were that day they'd stormed the garage and Val had pissed Mack off so much his face had turned redder than a boiled lobster.

Within twenty-four hours, they'd rounded up Nedra, Donna, Pastor Kind, the girl from the accident, and Mack's two thugs.

Nedra was the only one smart enough to pack her bags and scram that night at the church. She knew her hours were numbered. The police, however, found her in Salem after an all-points bulletin was released on her and her shiny new red Tesla.

Someone was commenting on the fact that the tapes would have to be reviewed and was quoted as saying that if he was the one to see those poor children recorded, he'd have a hard time not marching into that jail and stringing them all up by their wedding tackle. The

Sea Scroll even quoted him saying, "I hope Nedra, Kind, and the rest of those fuckweasels get it up the ass in more ways than one."

❖

Four days after Val had last gone to the police, Detective Randall called her back in.

Beyond the fodder she'd been consuming from the daily *Sea Scroll*, she was anxious to know what was happening with the investigation.

Detective Randall took her to the same room where they'd first met.

When they sat, he said, "The tape you gave us couldn't be used as evidence due to the break in what we call the chain of custody."

"What's that exactly?"

"It's a court term. A piece of evidence has to be handled carefully and in a documentable manner, from the time of seizure to turnover, so the defense can't lodge allegations of tampering. We can't prove the tape you gave us wasn't altered in any way."

"But I didn't alter it."

"I understand, but there's no way to prove that. We didn't want that tape to be eliminated as evidence. What we did do, however, is retrieve the rest of the tapes at Mack's. Those were properly handled and used so we have all we need.

"We've contacted the families and all the children are okay. They've had medical exams. They'll need counseling, of course, and continued support, but luckily no one was gravely injured."

"I'm glad they're all safe now."

Detective Randall nodded. "We had officers go out and question the neighbors who live around the church. Two different individuals witnessed the fight in the parking lot that night."

Val held her breath as a sudden wave of panic swept through her. She believed Cam had told her the truth, but that saying about the hard death of old habits rang in her ears.

"Both said that Mack not only started it, but Cam never had a chance to fight back. They also saw the two other men attack her, as well. Those charges will be added to their long lists."

"And Cam?"

"She's being processed out right now. If you'd like, you can go to the release area and wait for her. She'll need a ride home."

Val's heart soared and almost burst from her chest. Standing quickly, she said, "Thank you, Detective Randall. Thank you so much." She paused and quickly said, "Oh, I'm sorry. Is there anything else?"

He smiled at her. "Not for now."

"Thank you, again." She shook his hand.

"You risked a lot to do this. Some of the things you did weren't smart, but I think you know that."

"I do. I'm sorry."

He squeezed her hand for one last shake before releasing it. "Good work, though."

CHAPTER TWENTY-TWO

Cam rounded the corner and entered the Hemlock jail release area. She held a thick manila envelope and wore the same clothes she'd had on that night at the church. They were dirty, with streaks and stains of dark, dried blood on large parts of her shirt.

"Oh, shit," Val said as she rushed to Cam and threw her arms around her.

"That bad, huh?"

"No, no," Val said quickly but leaned away from her to examine her injuries. The cuts on Cam's forehead were now bandaged. Her cheeks were no longer swollen, but bruises ranging from purple to dark blue dotted her face, and her poor lower lip hung a little lower, still puffy from the blow she'd received there. Her one bad eye had opened slightly, but both were still bloodshot and blackened.

"Have you seen a doctor?"

"Someone came by the first night."

"Are you okay to walk?"

"I'm fine."

Val studied her for a sign of pain or dizziness. "Are you sure?"

"I'm sure I'd like to get the hell out of here, actually."

"Oh! I'm sorry, of course!" Val turned and put her arm around Cam, walking her out to the car.

As they drove back to the candy store, Cam kept fairly quiet, mostly looking out the window. Val reached out and put her hand over Cam's, but she only tightened her grip on Val's fingers slightly.

When Val parked in front of the shop, Cam got out of the car and opened the envelope. She pulled her keys out as Val met her on the sidewalk.

"Thanks for picking me up," Cam said. She sounded so small and fatigued.

"I'm coming up with you," Val said. She wouldn't take anything less than acquiescence as a reply.

"I..." Cam looked at her, and a sense of complete defeat seemed to radiate from her entire body.

"Cam," she said as she gently took the keys from her, "you don't need to say or do anything. I'm going to get you upstairs and make sure you're okay."

She watched for a response and had no idea if Cam was mad at her or happy to see her or simply done with her.

"Okay."

Val got Cam settled on the couch and went into the kitchen. Opening the fridge, she bypassed the milk, not knowing how old it now was, and scanned the rest of the offerings.

"Beer, water, or Coke?"

"Beer, please."

Val twisted the caps off two bottles and carried them over to the couch. She sat and they drank in silence. Val's brain was racing with a million things she wanted to say. She'd had a lot of time to think since the night at the church, especially since Cam had told her she wasn't involved in any of the shit they'd witnessed.

Surely Cam had had time to think, but Val had no idea where those thoughts had gone and what conclusions she'd reached. Understandably, she was decompressing from her incarceration, and Lord knew how much pain she felt.

Hours seemed to pass while Val waited, listening to the cars drive by on the highway below. Seagulls screeched every so often, and the voices of people walking by on the sidewalk outside drifted up to them like the nattering of office workers around a water dispenser.

Finally Cam tilted her head back, draining the last of her beer, and set the bottle down on the coffee table.

"The 45th parallel," Cam said. "What a place."

Val wasn't sure what she meant or how to respond.

"Nothing is ever exactly halfway." Cam held her hand up, moving it around in a slow circle. "A roulette wheel has red and black numbers to bet on, but it has a couple of green numbers that can throw everything off.

"And I've never done anything halfway in my life." She looked at Val. "When this town hated my family, I rebelled against that fact with all I had. When I decided to start my own business, I went full force. And when I met you, I would have done anything for you."

Val put her beer bottle down and waited again because it seemed like Cam wasn't finished.

"I'm sorry, Val, for getting you in trouble. You didn't deserve anything that happened to you, but I shouldn't have let you break into Mack's and I shouldn't have let you go to the church. I dragged you down, and that was wrong. I never intended—"

Val took her hand. "Cam, stop. You're not the one who should apologize." She placed her other hand on her chest. "I'm the one who needs to say I'm sorry."

Cam began to interrupt but Val shook her head. "I thought you were lying to me. I didn't believe you. After all you did to help me, I turned away from you and decided you couldn't be trusted. That's my M.O., Cam. I can't see past my own upbringing and fears.

"There you were, arms wide open, and I ran from you at the first sign that acceptance appeared to be inconsistent. That's because deep down I was looking for it. And guess what?" She laughed at herself. "I found it. At least I thought I found it. But I was dead wrong."

She turned her leg onto the couch, resting on the side of her knee, so she could face Cam. "I'm the one who has to apologize. Not you. You got beaten because of me. I am so, so sorry."

It was Cam's turn to chuckle. "I didn't scare you away, then?"

"My God, no."

"So are you saying your 45th parallel mug isn't cursed?"

Val caressed her swollen cheek. "Not in the slightest."

"What happens now?"

"I need to stay in town during the investigation, and I may get arrested for breaking into Mack's."

"Shit, Val," Cam said.

"It's fine. I told them I was the only one, though. They didn't need to know you were there, not after all you've been through. Mack may say you were, but he won't have any proof. That's one thing I can keep you from, and I will.

"I'll get a lawyer and hopefully the charges will be dropped. But even if they aren't, I don't care. My mom wanted something to be done about Nedra and the rest, and we were able to stop them. You and I."

"I like the way that last part sounds."

Val leaned toward her and they kissed softly. This was where Val wanted to be. Cam had her heart and would protect it.

Cam was her fresh pine. She could close her eyes and take in all that this woman had to give and then give all of herself in return.

"I love you," Val said.

Tears had come to Cam's eyes. "I love you too, Val."

Val wrapped her arms around her and held her.

The future had never been too forthcoming, and while it was still a huge unknown—what the police would do, what geographic challenges would arise—she had no doubt that she wanted to be with Cam.

"When this craziness is over," Cam said as her head rested against Val's, "may we go out on our very first date?"

"Wasn't the other night, in the backseat of Mr. Harlin's car, our first date?"

Val felt Cam jiggle against her body as she chuckled.

"All right, may we go out on our very first date when no one's out to kill us?"

"That clarifies your request much better." She brought her fingers up under Cam's chin, raising her beautiful face to hers. Before they kissed again, she said, "And the answer is yes."

About the Author

Lisa Girolami has been in the entertainment industry since 1979. Her tenure includes ten years as a production executive in the motion picture industry and another two-plus decades producing and designing theme parks for Disney and Universal Studios. She is now a Director and Senior Producer with Walt Disney Imagineering.

She received both her bachelor of arts degree and master's in psychology from the California State University, Long Beach. She is a licensed marriage and family therapist with the California Board of Behavioral Sciences.

She serves on the board of the Lambda Literary Foundation.

Residing in Long Beach, CA, with her wife, Kari, they happily share their abode with cats Pierre, Penelope, Jersey, and Mama Kitty; a dog named Tessa; and Clyde, the desert tortoise.

Books Available from Bold Strokes Books

The 45th Parallel by Lisa Girolami. Burying her mother isn't the worst thing that can happen to Val Montague when she returns to the woodsy but peculiar town of Hemlock, Oregon. (978-1-62639-342-4)

A Royal Romance by Jenny Frame. In a country where class still divides, can love topple the last social taboo and allow Queen Georgina and Beatrice Elliot, a working class girl, their happy ever after? (978-1-62639-360-8)

Bouncing by Jaime Maddox. Basketball Coach Alex Dalton has been bouncing from woman to woman, because no one ever held her interest, until she meets her new assistant, Britain Dodge. (978-1-62639-344-8)

Same Time Next Week by Emily Smith. A chance encounter between Alex Harris and the beautiful Michelle Masters leads to a whirlwind friendship, and causes Alex to question everything she's ever known—including her own marriage. (978-1-62639-345-5)

All Things Rise by Missouri Vaun. Cole rescues a striking pilot who crash-lands near her family's farm, setting in motion a chain of events that will forever alter the course of her life. (978-1-62639-346-2)

Riding Passion by D. Jackson Leigh. Mount up for the ride through a sizzling anthology of chance encounters, buried desires, romantic surprises, and blazing passion. (978-1-62639-349-3)

Love's Bounty by Yolanda Wallace. Lobster boat captain Jake Myers stopped living the day she cheated death, but meeting greenhorn Shy Silva stirs her back to life. (978-1-62639-334-9)

Just Three Words by Melissa Brayden. Sometimes the one you want is the one you least suspect. Accountant Samantha Ennis has her ordered life disrupted when heartbreaker Hunter Blair moves into her trendy Soho loft. (978-1-62639-335-6)

Lay Down the Law by Carsen Taite. Attorney Peyton Davis returns to her Texas roots to take on big oil and the Mexican Mafia, but will her investigation thwart her chance at true love? (978-1-62639-336-3)

Playing in Shadow by Lesley Davis. Survivor's guilt threatens to keep Bryce trapped in her nightmare world unless Scarlet's love can pull her out of the darkness back into the light. (978-1-62639-337-0)

Soul Selecta by Gill McKnight. Soul mates are hell to work with. (978-1-62639-338-7)

The Revelation of Beatrice Darby by Jean Copeland. Adolescence is complicated, but Beatrice Darby is about to discover how impossible it can seem to a lesbian coming of age in conservative 1950s New England. (978-1-62639-339-4)

Twice Lucky by Mardi Alexander. For firefighter Mackenzie James and Dr. Sarah Macarthur, there's suddenly a whole lot more in life to understand, to consider, to risk…someone will need to fight for her life. (978-1-62639-325-7)

Shadow Hunt by L.L. Raand. With young to raise and her Pack under attack, Sylvan, Alpha of the wolf Weres, takes on her greatest challenge when she determines to uncover the faceless enemies known as the Shadow Lords. A Midnight Hunters novel. (978-1-62639-326-4)

Heart of the Game by Rachel Spangler. A baseball writer falls for a single mom, but can she ever love anything as much as she loves the game? (978-1-62639-327-1)

Getting Lost by Michelle Grubb. Twenty-eight days, thirteen European countries, a tour manager fighting attraction, and an accused murderer: Stella and Phoebe's journey of a lifetime begins here. (978-1-62639-328-8)

Prayer of the Handmaiden by Merry Shannon. Celibate priestess Kadrian must defend the kingdom of Ithyria from a dangerous enemy and ultimately choose between her duty to the Goddess and the love of her childhood sweetheart, Erinda. (978-1-62639-329-5)

The Witch of Stalingrad by Justine Saracen. A Soviet "night witch" pilot and American journalist meet on the Eastern Front in WW II and struggle through carnage, conflicting politics, and the deadly Russian winter. (978-1-62639-330-1)

Pedal to the Metal by Jesse J. Thoma. When unreformed thief Dubs Williams is released from prison to help Max Winters bust a car theft ring, Max learns that to catch a thief, get in bed with one. (978-1-62639-239-7)

Dragon Horse War by D. Jackson Leigh. A priestess of peace and a fiery warrior must defeat a vicious uprising that entwines their destinies and ultimately their hearts. (978-1-62639-240-3)

For the Love of Cake by Erin Dutton. When everything is on the line, and one taste can break a heart, will pastry chefs Maya and Shannon take a chance on reality? (978-1-62639-241-0)

Betting on Love by Alyssa Linn Palmer. A quiet country-girl-at-heart and a live-life-to-the-fullest biker take a risk at offering each other their hearts. (978-1-62639-242-7)

The Deadening by Yvonne Heidt. The lines between good and evil, right and wrong, have always been blurry for Shade. When Raven's actions force her to choose, which side will she come out on? (978-1-62639-243-4)

Ordinary Mayhem by Victoria A. Brownworth. Faye Blakemore has been taking photographs since she was ten, but those same photographs threaten to destroy everything she knows and everything she loves. (978-1-62639-315-8)

One Last Thing by Kim Baldwin & Xenia Alexiou. Blood is thicker than pride. The final book in the Elite Operative Series brings together foes, family, and friends to start a new order. (978-1-62639-230-4)

Songs Unfinished by Holly Stratimore. Two aspiring rock stars learn that falling in love while pursuing their dreams can be harmonious—if they can only keep their pasts from throwing them out of tune. (978-1-62639-231-1)

Beyond the Ridge by L.T. Marie. Will a contractor and a horse rancher overcome their family differences and find common ground to build a life together? (978-1-62639-232-8)

Swordfish by Andrea Bramhall. Four women battle the demons from their pasts. Will they learn to let go, or will happiness be forever beyond their grasp? (978-1-62639-233-5)

The Fiend Queen by Barbara Ann Wright. Princess Katya and her consort Starbride must turn evil against evil in order to banish Fiendish power from their kingdom, and only love will pull them back from the brink. (978-1-62639-234-2)

Up the Ante by PJ Trebelhorn. When Jordan Stryker and Ashley Noble meet again fifteen years after a short-lived affair, are either of them prepared to gamble on a chance at love? (978-1-62639-237-3)

Speakeasy by MJ Williamz. When mob leader Helen Byrne sets her sights on the girlfriend of Al Capone's right-hand man, passion and tempers flare on the streets of Chicago. (978-1-62639-238-0)

Venus in Love by Tina Michele. Morgan Blake can't afford any distractions and Ainsley Dencourt can't afford to lose control—but the beauty of life and art usually lies in the unpredictable strokes of the artist's brush. (978-1-62639-220-5)

Rules of Revenge by AJ Quinn. When a lethal operative on a collision course with her past agrees to help a CIA analyst on a critical assignment, the encounter proves explosive in ways neither woman anticipated. (978-1-62639-221-2)

The Romance Vote by Ali Vali. Chili Alexander is a sought-after campaign consultant who isn't prepared when her boss's daughter, Samantha Pellegrin, comes to work at the firm and shakes up Chili's life from the first day. (978-1-62639-222-9)

Advance: Exodus Book One by Gun Brooke. Admiral Dael Caydoc's mission to find a new homeworld for the Oconodian people is hazardous, but working with the infuriating Commander Aniwyn "Spinner" Seclan endangers her heart and soul. (978-1-62639-224-3)

UnCatholic Conduct by Stevie Mikayne. Jil Kidd goes undercover to investigate fraud at St. Marguerite's Catholic School, but life gets complicated when her student is killed—and she begins to fall for her prime target. (978-1-62639-304-2)

Season's Meetings by Amy Dunne. Catherine Birch reluctantly ventures on the festive road trip from hell with beautiful stranger Holly Daniels only to discover the road to true love has its own obstacles to maneuver. (978-1-62639-227-4)

Myth and Magic: Queer Fairy Tales edited by Radclyffe and Stacia Seaman. Myth, magic, and monsters—the stuff of childhood dreams (or nightmares) and adult fantasies. (978-1-62639-225-0)

Nine Nights on the Windy Tree by Martha Miller. Recovering drug addict, Bertha Brannon, is an attorney who is trying to stay clean when a murder sends her back to the bad end of town. (978-1-62639-179-6)

Driving Lessons by Annameekee Hesik. Dive into Abbey Brooks's sophomore year as she attempts to figure out the amazing, but sometimes complicated, life of a you-know-who girl at Gila High School. (978-1-62639-228-1)

Asher's Shot by Elizabeth Wheeler. Asher Price's candid photographs capture the truth, but when his success requires exposing an enemy, Asher discovers his only shot at happiness involves revealing secrets of his own. (978-1-62639-229-8)

Courtship by Carsen Taite. Love and justice—a lethal mix or a perfect match? (978-1-62639-210-6)

Against Doctor's Orders by Radclyffe. Corporate financier Presley Worth wants to shut down Argyle Community Hospital, but Dr. Harper Rivers will fight her every step of the way, if she can also fight their growing attraction. (978-1-62639-211-3)

A Spark of Heavenly Fire by Kathleen Knowles. Kerry and Beth are building their life together, but unexpected circumstances could destroy their happiness. (978-1-62639-212-0)

Never Too Late by Julie Blair. When Dr. Jamie Hammond is forced to hire a new office manager, she's shocked to come face to face with Carla Grant and memories from her past. (978-1-62639-213-7)

Widow by Martha Miller. Judge Bertha Brannon must solve the murder of her lover, a policewoman she thought she'd grow old with. As more bodies pile up, the murderer starts coming for her. (978-1-62639-214-4)

Twisted Echoes by Sheri Lewis Wohl. What's a woman to do when she realizes the voices in her head are real? (978-1-62639-215-1)